MCCULLOUGH'S JAMBOREE BOOK 5

KATHI S. BARTON

This is a work of fiction. Names, characters, places, and incidents are products of the author's imagination or are used fictitiously and are not to be construed as real. Any resemblance to actual events, locations, organizations, or persons, living or dead, is entirely coincidental.

World Castle Publishing, LLC
Pensacola, Florida
Copyright © Kathi S. Barton 2018
Paperback ISBN: 9781629899305
eBook ISBN: 9781629899312
First Edition World Castle Publishing, LLC, May 28, 2018
http://www.worldcastlepublishing.com
Licensing Notes
Cover: Karen Fuller
Editor: Maxine Bringenberg

Table of Contents

Chapter 1

Lauren didn't like not having answers. She supposed that was an understatement, but things just weren't adding up for her. As she began writing down what she knew and what she didn't, the sticky notes began taking on a bizarre color scheme that only she could figure out. When Colin came into the office with her, she stood and started sticking them on the wall with the pictures that she'd hung up.

"Are these the people that you've been searching for?" She told him that the world was searching for them, it seemed. "Yes, well, whoever they are, they're wanted in four countries, you told me, and that wasn't even counting the countries that they've not been found out in."

"Yes, well, I'm working on that one too. There are several deaths that I can have tagged to them, but nothing to stick so far." She hung up the notes and then stepped back. "Things aren't adding up in their usual fucking order like I like them to do."

"Hawk was just here. He said to tell you that he'd be back in a couple of days. It's too much for him. I have no idea what that is supposed to mean either." She told him. "How can we be driving him insane when he doesn't hang around us all that much now? I mean, he was in here for about two minutes before he took off again. How am I supposed to be driving him crazy?"

"You're around. And don't ask me questions if all you're going to do is try and prove to me why I'm not right. We both know that I am, and the sooner you get that in your thick skull, the better off you're going to be." They both laughed. "What do you see when you look at this?"

He had helped her a few times when she'd had something staring her right in the face over the last few months. Mostly it was because he was fresh eyes and wasn't tainted by her jadedness. And she knew that she was. Lauren didn't trust anyone, and didn't like people twice as much as her trust level was. Colin got up and looked over the board.

"The blue notes, what are they?" She told him they were facts. "And the yellow ones? I'm assuming you have this color coded. It'll help me to figure it out if I know it all."

"Yellow is for unknown factors. Such as I don't know how the fuck they're being funded. The blue ones are place markers. As you can see I've only put numbers on them. The questions are eluding me as well." He nodded, and he continued to look over her board of pictures and notes. "The red ones are names that I know that they've killed. And as you can see, some of them are straddled between two names. So I'm not entirely sure what I'm looking at here."

"Is it the same person that might have killed the ones you

6

have straddled between two names?" She looked at the board and asked him what he meant. "The people that you have under two names. You think they might have been killed by two different people. Maybe it's just one person that looks like two to throw you off. I mean, are you sure that they're not one and the same murderer?"

"Why do you ask that? I'm not saying that you're wrong, but I never thought of that yet." She looked at the traits of both men and women on her list. They were similar, but not terribly so. But when Colin pointed out that the names were nearly the same, she then noticed a few other things about them as well.

"This one stays in the same type of hotel. High end and lots of room service. They always go out for drinks with their intended victim before taking them back to the room to murder them." She took down the second picture but laid it aside. She didn't know which one the right person was, but it was getting easier to see them now. "These two people always wear a wig that is made not from manmade hair, but of different animals. The only reason we know this is because the latest victim pulled out a lot of their hair when he was trying to defend himself. He had a lot of defensive wounds."

"These two have the same initials as well." She nodded and put the picture with the other one. "Don't you think these are the same picture?"

"I thought that as well, but I've concluded that they're not. Unless they've had some work done since the first one was taken." She showed him the nose and how it was shaped, and the lips. "I guess they could have had collagen put in, but I don't know how that affects the body as well as say, a doctor would. I've called Boyd over to look at them."

Lauren was a mess working on this one. It was something that she'd pulled from the cold files at the police station. She wasn't working for Jarvis as much right now—he was trying to close his end of being president right now. He still had two years to go, but he wasn't running for reelection, so she wasn't sure what she was supposed to do now and when he was finished. She told Colin what she was thinking.

"I thought you were a lifer." She said that she'd be a dead one if she didn't have something to do soon. "Yeah, I figured that was why you asked for the files to be sent over. If you want, I can show you how to use a sander and you can help us out."

"No thanks. I have all my fingers just where I want them." She moved a few of the folders and sat down. "I've talked to Boyd about Sandy, and he said that she's not his mate. They get along well but decided that they're not going to be involved. I had no idea that he'd lost his mate years ago."

"I didn't know either until he told us at dinner a couple of weeks ago. He said that she was a student at the college when he was. But he'd had his head so buried in studying that he didn't notice her until it was too late." She asked him if there was a chance that he could have been wrong about the other woman. "No, I don't think so. He knew it was her. Had the overwhelming need to be with her but knew that he had to study too. Then when he came out of his study session one night, she'd been killed by a hit and run driver. Mom took it very hard too, I think."

Bea had too. And so had Rich. He must have told their son he was sorry a thousand times at dinner, then had to go out on the deck to get himself under control. Rich wanted his kids to be happy, and thought that having a mate, each of them, was the only way they were going to be. Victoria had come to her last night and answered a few questions about mates, things that she hadn't wanted to ask Colin about. Like could they get a second chance sometimes.

"Yes, anyone can. But I have a feeling that our young Boyd doesn't care to look for it." Lauren had asked her why. "He's so set in his ways, don't you think? I mean, it's like he's found her, she's gone, and that's all she wrote. The guy could be a poster child for anal retentive men."

"I don't think he's that bad, but I do see your point." Lauren thought of his office as compared to her own. "He puts me to shame every time he has to come here. He tisks at me like an old woman and tells me that I should have more respect for my things. I just put my gun on the table and tell him I do, for the ones that could save my life."

When Colin left her to go back to his job of working with his brother and dad, she sat down at her desk and looked around her office. There wasn't much more she could do on this, but she knew that sooner rather than later, she'd figure it out. Since she was working on several other things now, she thought about Christmas which was in two weeks.

There were decorations all over the house right now. A great many of them were where they should have been, gracing the staircase or hanging on the tree, but other things were still in boxes and hadn't been put up. Lauren was excited to have a family Christmas. It would be her first one in a very long time.

The tree alone had her coming downstairs in the middle

of the night and turning it on. The decorations on it, all of them, twinkled around the room like a sparkler on the Fourth. Then there were the packages, more every day, that were under it. She'd not gone snooping in them—she knew what they were…they were for their children. But she was just as excited as any child for this coming holiday.

They were going to have Christmas Eve at their own houses, with their own families, then on the big morning they were headed to Colin's parents' house, her parents too, to have a long, fun day with them. Then there was food all day, as well as massive amounts of football. She herself had fallen in love with the sport long before she knew that his entire family would schedule a meal around their favorite teams.

Looking at the time, she gathered up what she needed and waited for Boyd to come over. He and Mac were closing the clinic after today to take a much-needed vacation. Mac and Dustin were planning a nice getaway after the holiday, and she and Colin were going to spend a couple of days in Washington with Jarvis. She'd never spent a holiday with the president before and thought it might be fun. At least she wouldn't be working the entire time.

Boyd showed up about half an hour later, saying that he'd just delivered his one hundredth baby. The man was a wonder, she'd give him that. One hundred babies brought into the world, and he acted like it was the first time every time. Smiling, she brought him into her office to work and loved that he didn't disappoint her in pointing out what a slob she was. Boyd could make her laugh quicker than any of the McCullough men.

~~~

After Boyd and Lauren finished up his help to her, they sat at the big desk and looked over the work she was doing now. He couldn't offer her any help on her notes and pictures, but he did tell her that the two people in the picture were one and the same. He said that she'd have to learn eyes. Not that she didn't know a great deal about people, but the eyes never lied to you.

"I've been looking at houses. Dustin is helping me find something reasonable." Lauren asked him if he was looking for big. "I wasn't, but there isn't much of a choice in the smaller houses that I was looking for. He said that bigger is better."

"Yeah, he would. I was noticing the house that they're working on now. That's a little bitty thing, at least compared to all the houses that the rest of them own." Boyd laughed with her. He told her that the house was sold already. "That was fast. I had no idea that it was even on the market yet."

"It's not, but they were working on it the day before yesterday and a couple came in to look around. Before they knew it, they were picking out carpet colors and paint colors for them. I guess they got a loan yesterday, and now they're working with them to make it their home."

"That's good for them, I guess. Why smaller, if you don't mind me asking?" Boyd had been telling his family that he wouldn't have a mate coming his way. He had told his family so far, and decided that he might as well tell everyone else too. He mentioned it again to Lauren. "I'm sorry, Boyd. I never thought that you guys could just not take your mate. And you told us that she was killed too. That really sucks. But in talking with Victoria, she said that there is always a chance that you could find another mate. It has happened before."

11

"I know. I thought I had plenty of time. I guess I do now, but I no longer have anyone to spend it with." He didn't like feeling sorry for himself, and tried to think of something to talk about. Anything else but a mate. "I should get going. I know you have a lot of work going on here."

"Actually, I'm just helping out on some cold cases for the moment. You and your brothers, you all have contributed something to the cause. I'm just biding my time until something comes along with Jarvis. But I have solved one of them so far." He asked her about it. "They thought it was a robbery gone bad, but I found receipts in the man's things that said that he'd sold off all his worldly goods then killed himself. A good job of it too, meaning that he did it in a way that really did point to murder."

"And what does it matter? I'm not belittling your work—I think it's fantastic. But what does it matter to the system if he's murdered or killed himself?" She handed him a sheet of paper, and on it were the same names and dates. "I don't understand this."

"Insurance claims. They want his insurance, and if he was murdered, it would have been doubled. I was asked to figure out if I could find the murderer. Instead, I found that he killed himself. They'll not get it now." He told her that he thought that was sort of sad, and cruel too. "Yes, it is. And I agree with you that he fucked over his family. But that's the truth of the matter, and that's what I found. Now the case is closed, and no more man hours will be wasted on it."

"Do you think that was his purpose in making it all neat and tidy?" Lauren nodded. "All right, I guess, but he must have had his reasons, that's all I'm saying."

"I'm sure that he did." She shoved the file under the other files on her desk and Boyd stood up. "You want some help house hunting? I'm about done here, and I could use a break. And if you're really nice to me, which I don't know why you wouldn't be, I'll let you buy me lunch."

"Sounds good to me." They were out the door and in his car before he realized that he hadn't been planning on house hunting today. "Dustin hasn't lined up any houses for me to look at. I have nowhere to go."

"I know. But you seemed sort of down and I needed to get out. We'll wing it." Boyd stared at his sister-in-law. "All right, all right, I know I don't wing it well, but I really did need to get out of the house. So, where do we start? I'm thinking that we hit a realtor and go from there."

The office of the only agent in town wasn't busy, and he was able to get someone to give him a list rather than follow them around all afternoon. Boyd supposed that it was because of Lauren. She'd said no, they didn't need the realtor to go with them, and no one disputed her claim that they had this. He was still laughing at the expression on the woman's face when Lauren told her no. He'd bet few people told her that and got away with it. Much like Lauren.

They hit two houses before they stopped for lunch. The first one had too much work that needed to be done on it. And Dustin had already told him that he had five houses that he had to work on before summer, as they were homes for vets. Dustin and their family did that when they could, helped injured vets with homes that would suit their needs.

They were eating their lunch as they looked over the map they'd been given. Lauren crossed two of the dozen or so

13

houses off the list right away. She said they were too far from the family for him to think about purchasing them.

"Perhaps I don't want to live close to all of you." She snorted at him. "You know, you're not as pleasant to be around as you might think. I mean, I've had wild cats with more friendliness than you display all the time."

"Yes, but I can save your ass if you need it, and you know that I will tell you the truth, even if you don't want to hear it. But I can also lie right to your face and you'd never know." He asked her how she thought that was a good thing. "It is. Like the shirt you have on. I could have said to you, Christ, Boyd, that's a shirt an old man would wear. And you'd change. But I held my tongue."

Boyd looked down at his polo and then back at her. "What's wrong with this shirt? You have one on that is just the same. Only mine is blue and yours is black. By the way, do you own any other color than black?"

"No, I don't. And you could use some color in your life too. I'm too set in my ways to change my style. But you, you should wear colors." He pointed out that blue was a color. "Nah, it's a mood. Blue is a mood. You should wear green or yellow. You'd look good in yellow."

He didn't even know what to say to her. There were times when he had no idea if she was giving him a hard time or not. Like her being able to lie to him and he wouldn't know if she was telling him a lie or the truth. So instead of engaging with her, he ate his burger and fries. Before he was finishing off his malt, she had marked two more off the list and had circled four of them.

Paying for lunch, he looked around the diner. It was a

place he'd been coming to since he'd been a kid. And it really hadn't changed all that much. In two weeks the new owner, Reese, would close it down and have the entire place updated, expanded, as well as adding an ice cream area for the local kids. This was all done on the sly — she wouldn't know it was hers until Christmas morning. Jon and Parker had bought it for her.

"You think they'll keep the bar stools?" Lauren asked him why he'd want them. "I don't know. It's something that the six of us would sit on when my parents would bring us here for a treat. There used to be a soda fountain machine in here until it died with the old ways. I guess I'm a little nostalgic for my childhood."

Lauren popped him in the back of the head. "Get over it. You need to focus on the here and now, my dear brother. And when you get a house, I expect to get full credit for you buying it. Even if you have to lie about it."

They were still laughing as they made their way to the next house. He didn't care for the neighborhood, but he was willing to give it a chance. But the closer they got to the place, the more uncomfortable he felt — like dread or the feeling of impending pain. When he sat in the car, just staring up at the house, Lauren asked him what was wrong.

"I don't know. I can feel something here." She asked if it was just what he'd been thinking, and he turned to her. "You feel it too then?"

"Yes. Like I'm going to open that door and sixty men with guns and knives are going to come out and fuck up my wonderful day. I hate having to kill someone before dinner. It gives me heartburn." He asked her what she thought it did to the people she killed. "I never thought of that, not that I care, but I never thought of that. Thanks."

Instead of moving on to the next house, they got out to see what was making them feel like that. As soon as they stepped up on the porch, the smell of fresh blood flooded his nose. He looked over at Lauren when she cursed. She pulled out her gun and he stood there as she took her booted foot and slammed it against the doorway.

The stronger smell hit his nostrils first. Blood and a great deal of it. Then he could feel something akin to sorrow. Boyd stayed by the door when he was told to and waited for her to tell him to move. But before he could reach out to his brothers, not even sure what they were going to be needed for, he saw the movement near the stairs and nearly ran toward it when Lauren stopped him.

"Do you know what stay here means?" He said that he did and pointed to what had moved. "It had better be something more than a dead rat or I'm kicking your ass all the way to the car. This is not how a person finds them a house."

Not only wasn't it a dead rat, though he had seen it move so that ruled it out right away, but it was a body. A man's body that was still breathing, though barely so. As he told Lauren to go and get his medical bag out of his car, he started assessing the man for injuries. The blood was everywhere, and he seemed to be bleeding from every part of his body.

"What's your name?" The man moaned and pointed to the stairs. Looking up, Boyd could see that he might have come through the railing. He didn't tell him his name, and Boyd began searching for any kind of identification on him.

"What the fuck are you doing?" He told her that he was

looking for alert bracelets or even a necklace that said maybe he had something else wrong with him. "Another thing I wouldn't have thought of. But then, I don't know that many people that I'd care enough about to check on that."

He knew that she was kidding around. There were plenty of people in her life that she loved enough to check for things like this. And Boyd was pretty sure that he was one of them. When he found that the man was on a blood thinner, he tried his best to find the biggest source of blood loss. Even small cuts could make him bleed more than usual.

About the time he got the IV in, the paramedics showed up. Boyd knew that even though they'd gotten to him fast enough, he still might die from his injuries. He had a feeling that the man was lucky they'd not driven off and had stuck around to inspect the house. Boyd rode to the hospital with the man while Lauren talked to the police. The house, it seemed, wasn't going to be one that he'd buy anytime soon, if ever.

Chapter 2

Reilly didn't want to be bothered, and when someone knocked on her door after she put her phone on mute, she told them to go away. She just knew that it was going to be her boss again, and she didn't want to deal with his grabby hands and caustic mouth. Not today.

"You're to call the hospital." She looked at Lesley when she opened the door and poked her head in. "Something to do with your dad. I think he's been taken there."

Picking up her phone, she dialed the number to her dad's cell. When it went to voice mail, she grabbed her things and made her way to the door, asking Lesley what she knew, which was nothing. And just as she was making her way to the door, her boss decided to come out of his office.

"Where are you going?" She told him that her dad had been hurt. "So? You have reports that I need for a court date tomorrow, and I told you that you weren't leaving until they were finished. Unless, of course, you want to show me a good

19

time and I'll have someone else do them."

He wasn't even trying to be discreet anymore. Ross would grab her ass when she walked by him, and no amount of threats about going to his dad helped her. Mr. Dander, the senior, would just wave her off and tell her to keep away from Ross. Like that fucking ever worked.

"No, I do not want to show you a good time. My father is ill, and I need to go to him." Ross stood there with his arms over his chest like a small child. Ignoring him for the doorway, she was nearly to it when he called her name.

"You leave, and I will consider this job abandonment. You know that I can do it too, and fire your ass. Then where will your precious father be with you unemployed?" She thought about it, what her options were, and said fuck it. She was out the door before she could give a thought to what the fuck she was really doing.

Her car barely started, but when it did, she sat there for several minutes just to get her bearing on what she'd done. Backing out of the parking place, she turned to go forward when something slammed into her rear end. Turning around, she couldn't believe that Ross was there, his hands beating on her trunk like a madman. She glanced at her video recorder and was glad to see that it was on. No one would believe her if she tried to tell them what he'd done.

He came to her window then and started pounding on it as well, screaming at her that he wanted her to get back inside, that he was going to kill her. Reilly didn't roll it down all the way, just an inch, and asked him what he thought he was doing. Ross had become unhinged a great deal lately, and she was sort of afraid of him.

"You will get your ass back to your desk and leave when I tell you that you can." She said that she was quitting. "Like you're going to be able to do that either. I'm serious, Reilly. You aren't making this easy on yourself. Get in there and do your job, or I swear to you, I'll kill you. And enjoy it too. Get out of this car."

He pounded on the window and she put it in reverse again and started backing up slowly, the entire time yelling at him that she had quit and that she was leaving. By the time she had turned around enough to leave, the entire staff was outside now, watching what he was doing to her and her car. A lot of them had their cell phones out recording it. Reilly could not believe that none of them had come to help her. It showed her just how much she meant to them.

When she was pulling out of the parking lot and onto the main road, Reilly drove for another few blocks before she had to pull over. Getting out, she almost didn't make it to the grassy area beside the highway before she was throwing up. Christ. Just going down on her knees in the soft grass made her feel a little better.

Just as she was headed to her car to go to the hospital, a little black sports car came out of nowhere and rammed her car in the rear. It hit so hard that her car went off the side of the road into oncoming traffic on the freeway that was going at least sixty to seventy miles per hour. As soon as her car slammed into the side of the first car, it was a free for all. The cars kept hitting one another, and there was nothing she could do about it but watch.

Reilly cringed as car after car slammed into her car. The carnage that was caused had her flinching each time brakes

21

squealed, and horns blared. And the whole time, the little black car sat on the side of the road where it had hit her, and the driver gunned the engine. Taking out her cell phone, she recorded the reactions of the accident as well as the man when he got out of the car. It was Ross.

He was jumping up and down, laughing. Even as far away as she was, she could hear him shouting about how he'd done it, he'd killed her. She wondered if he knew that she wasn't in the car and backed up, careful of where she stepped. She was afraid that he'd come after her, to somehow finish the job.

He was insane. Something was seriously wrong with him, she thought. And when he started taking pictures of what was going on, she turned and ran to the other side of the road and flagged down the first car that she saw. The limo didn't just stop, but the woman in the back got out of the car with a gun drawn.

"He pushed me into the traffic. Like I was nothing more than a.... I don't know what he thought he was doing, but I could have been killed. He said that, that he'd killed me, like it was the joy of his life." The woman started forward toward where the accident was still going on, and Reilly had to stop her. No more people needed to be hurt by the madman. "Please. Don't. If you let him see me then he'll come after us both. I don't want you hurt because he's fucking insane right now."

The woman pulled out her phone and called the police, she thought. When she told them who she was, Hutch something, Reilly leaned against the car and watched as people began to get out of their cars and look at the damage. There must have been fifty cars that were in some kind of crumpled mess. And it wasn't over. There were more cars coming around the small bend in the highway, and none of them had enough time to stop.

The woman told her to get in the car and to not get out until she told her to. Grabbing for the door, thinking that she was safer hidden away, Reilly nearly sobbed with relief when she finally got the door open and slipped inside.

There was a man in the car with her, she noticed, and tried very hard not to stare at him. While she had dated some lately, the man sitting on the bench seat looked like he would be the envy of every other male in the world. When he chuckled slightly, she glared at him.

"My wife, Lauren, she'll keep you safe." Nodding, she told him her name. "Hello, Reilly Pratt. I'm Colin McCullough, and my wife's name is Lauren. We were just headed home from the hospital when our driver saw you. Were you hurt at all in this?"

"No, I'm okay. Terrified, but…. My father. I completely forgot him. He's been hurt. I have to go there." She reached for the door, and he stopped her with his hand over hers. "Look, buddy. While you have the body of an Adonis, I'm not going to have one more man handle me like day old bread again. Let go of me or I'll have to break your hand."

"I'm just going to remind you that you might not have a car right now, and my wife said not to move." She looked out the darkened window of the car. "If you will just give me a moment, I'll tell her that you need to go, and I'll come back for her."

"I can walk." Shaking his head, he told her to wait. "I can. I'm neither hurt nor am I lazy. I have to walk a lot when my car breaks down. I guess it's beyond broken now. Did you see what he did? He shoved my car into traffic like it was a fun day at the zoo for him." Reilly knew she was babbling again, and snapped her mouth closed.

"I'm sure it is, but for now, trust me when I say you'll be safer if I take you. Not to mention, you'll get there sooner instead of sometime tomorrow." Nodding, she waited for him. "Please, don't leave this car. I don't want you hurt either."

When he opened the door, she could hear the woman speaking to Ross. While she was loud, he was louder, saying that he'd had nothing to do with the car being in the road. The door shut on them when the woman, Lauren, started talking again.

As she sat there, waiting on the man, Colin, to return, she thought about the last twenty minutes. Ross had tried to kill her. There was no doubt that was what he'd been trying to do. He'd hit her car from the rear and had shoved it into oncoming traffic. She shivered when she thought of what would have happened to her had she been in the car when he'd done that. There was no doubt in her mind that she'd be dead, and he'd be jumping up and down like a fool because of it.

When Colin got back into the limo, he told the driver to take them to the hospital. She felt bad that he had to leave his wife and told him that. Reilly was terrified out of her mind, but she thought that he might have figured that one out on his own.

"This man, did the two of you have a fight? Is he a boyfriend?" She shook her head and told him that she'd worked for him until all this happened, then told him what Ross's name was. "Lauren said that he's saying that you drove yourself into the traffic, and that he hoped that you were dead."

"I wasn't in the car." He said he could see that. "I think had I been in the car, it would have killed me, don't you think?"

"Oh yeah, you'd be dead. That's why Lauren is having such a good time with Ross. Anyway, I'm to take you to the hospital and to tell you not to leave there until someone comes to get you. It'll more than likely be one of my brothers." Reilly told him she'd be fine there. There were other people around. "Yes, well, having others around didn't stop him this time from plowing you into a fifty-car pileup. Correct? Please, just do as we ask, and no one will come near you. We all look pretty much alike, so you won't have any trouble figuring out who we are, okay?"

Colin asked her some questions that made her think he might be a cop or something. She did tell him that there was a camera on her car, but it was probably smashed to hell by now. He told her that they might be able to get something from it. He also asked her what she did working for Ross.

"Research staff. I don't have any idea if there is a title for that or anything, but I'm pretty good at researching things. He wanted me to stay and work on the file he gave me, but my dad's been hurt. I was leaving when he told me that if I had sex with him, or in his words, gave him a good time, then he could have someone else work on them. Otherwise, I wasn't leaving." Colin said he sounded like a charmer. "He's a fucking dick. And when I went to his dad a while back, who is the actual attorney that I started working for, he waved me off. Like I was a pesky fly or something. He told me to avoid

Ross in the future. I can't do that, he's my fucking boss. I'm sorry."

"Don't worry about it, Reilly. You're upset, and I can understand that, but Ross is telling Lauren that you were pissed off because he turned down your advances, and that the two of you had had a one-night thing. He said that you were a great disappointment and he didn't want to see you again. But you persisted." She looked out the window and said nothing. "Reilly, I'm only telling you what he's saying, not that we believe him."

"It doesn't matter." The car came to a smooth stop and she reached for the handle again. Reilly turned to him before getting out of the car. "Thank you for bringing me here, Mr. McCullough. I do appreciate it."

"It was a pleasure, Miss Pratt. Remember what I said — don't leave here unless one of my brothers is with you. This Dander person is off his rocker." She nodded and told him that she was fine even as she got out of the car.

Going to the front desk, she asked about her dad. He was still in surgery, so she asked if there was anyone that she could talk to about what had happened. The woman there directed her to the police officer that was standing by the doors.

"Hello, miss. I'm to understand that you're here about your father?" She said that she was and told him his name. "I'm Joe Windfall. I'm the acting chief right now. I wanted to talk to you before you got to see your father. He was found in a house that is for sale around here. Did you know anything about that?"

"Yes. Well, sort of. He does woodworking for homes. Like replacement pieces for gingerbread work trim. Hardwood floors that might have a spot that needs to be replaced as well. Sometimes he's asked to go to houses and give an estimate on having the floors redone. He told me this morning that he'd been asked to see a house on Winding Row to see if the home was worth the asking price for the amount of work that might need to be done." Joe nodded at her. "What happened to him? I know only that he was hurt and is now in surgery."

"The best we can tell you right now is that a couple of friends of mine were looking at houses and came upon him laying at the bottom of a flight of stairs. We think that he fell over the top and landed there." She asked him if he was hurt badly. "Boyd, he was there, and he is a doctor. He started helping him right away. And he made sure to tell the surgeon that Mr. Pratt—Ronald, right?—that he was on blood thinners as well."

"Yes, that's his first name. My dad has some clotting issues and has only just started taking them regularly." Since she had moved in and made him, really. But she didn't tell the officer that. "Do you think he'll be all right? He's all I have in the world."

"I will tell you that he's with the best we have. Mac, the surgeon, is one hell of a doctor." She nodded and sat down in the chair then, her knees finally giving out on her. "Lauren said that you were to stay here. She said that a Mr. Dander was looking for you."

"He tried to kill me." Joe asked her if she was all right. "Yes. I wasn't in my car when he hit me. I have a recording on my phone where he danced around after cars started hitting mine. And there is a camera in my car, though I don't know if it's going to be usable or not."

27

The radio at his throat started squawking and she listened in while someone told him about the pile-up on the highway. When he said that he was on his way, she told him to be careful. When he left her, Reilly asked the nurses where the surgery floor was so that she could be there for her dad when he was finished up. After going to the basement, where the surgery floor was, she sat down in one of the ugliest chairs she'd ever seen and closed her eyes.

"What a fucking day." She was unemployed and had no car. Reilly wondered what more bad news could befall her today, and was almost afraid to think about what else might happen. Then she wondered if Ross really was going to come after her again.

~~~

Boyd was assisting Mac on the surgery. While she was doing her best to get his chest sewn up, he was stitching together all the other places on Mr. Pratt's body. And there were a great many places that he'd been cut when the wood had splintered as he fell atop it.

When he'd done all he could for his left leg, he moved to the right. The man was lucky in that he'd only broken his left arm in all this and not his back. His left side had taken the brunt of the fall, he surmised, and started stitching the top of his foot closed as Mac asked him what had happened with his house hunting.

"That's what we were doing when we found Mr. Pratt. He was in one of the houses." Mac glanced at him and asked if he was serious. "I am. Lauren and I weren't even going to go in—the house was sort of creepy to me for some reason. But we found him there as soon as we went in. I don't think he'd been there very long. Perhaps five minutes or less. He was still conscious, for a little while anyway."

"He's a lucky bastard. And the fact that you knew to tell us about his blood is all that might save his life." He thanked her as he finished up with the man's foot. "He'll be laid up for a little while. And then there will have to be some physical therapy. Does he have anyone?"

"A daughter, but when I was last talking to Lauren, she'd not talked to her as yet. Her workplace wasn't putting the call through or something. I think she said that if she was working there, she might well have knocked the shit out of the person who answered the second time she called." Boyd did wonder about a place that would tell someone calling in to go to hell. "I guess she was going over there when—"

The call over the intercom alerted them to a multiple car accident on the freeway. All hands that were free were to report to the emergency room. Boyd immediately reached out to Lauren to find out what was going on.

You should see this fucking mess I have here, Boyd. You guys are going to be busy for some time today. If you can, I'd call in extras — you're going to need it. He asked her what had happened. *Some moron tried to push a woman that, lucky for her, wasn't in her car into the highway. The car came down off one of the little side streets and into oncoming traffic. Caused a major pile up. I have four dead so far, and a semi that has flipped onto cars. I have no idea if there are more under it. Christ, it's a fucking mess. And the guy tried to tell me that he'd had nothing to do with it. He still thinks the woman was in her car and that she's dead. He's actually telling me that he hopes that she was in it. Like I said, one lucky woman.*

He stripped off his gown to be gowned again to go

29

to the ER. He was done sewing the man up, and he was needed elsewhere. As soon as he hit the department, the first ambulance was pulling up. The nurses were bringing in more supplies as he started to assess the trauma.

He worked until he couldn't. They were still coming in, some by car, others by ambulance. He had one man bring in three people in his pickup truck. It was the worst disaster he'd ever seen in all his years as a doctor. And when Mac joined them an hour later, she was sent back to the operating room to try and save a man who had hit his head against the window and shattered his skull.

Boyd had no idea of the time when they said that the last ambulance was coming in. They would still have to deal with the dead. As it was right now, they were sending them to the morgue without checking much more than pulse and blood pressure. They had sent a student to the area, just to make sure.

Standing in the long hall of the department, he took the bottle of orange juice when it was handed to him, as well as the package of graham crackers. Christ, he'd never been so tired in all his life.

There were so many people in the waiting area that he was almost afraid to ask them what they needed. There were volunteers there as well, some of them dressed in the blue smock that told you who they worked for. There were others in jeans and T-shirts. The one person that stood out in all of this mess was a woman with a clipboard, dressed in a business suit and heels. He had no idea how long she'd been there, but she looked as if her feet were killing her.

"Her dad is here. You and Mac operated on him before

this went to shit." He looked over at Lauren when she came up beside him, speaking. "She didn't know what to do, so one of the nurses asked her to get names and numbers of the people waiting to hear if their family was here. She's been doing it since I showed up about five hours ago."

"How is the clean up going out there? One of the injured that came in said that it would be days before the highway would be opened up again." She said that she'd called in some extra help. "Some of your friends came to help?"

"Yeah. Bear worked on cars in the Army, so he could drive a big tow truck. Got most of it off and out of the way in a couple of hours. Now it's just clean up. And that might be all night. Chickens are running around all over the place too. One of the rigs was carrying them. And Jon came to help us lift some of the heavier trucks off of cars." He nodded and asked her how many were killed. "There are ten dead. That many more that are critical, I was told, and I haven't any idea how many injured. This guy that I had arrested is screaming for his lawyer, and saying he's going to have me arrested too. I would welcome the cell about now, I think."

"Do you have any more information on what went down? Other than what you told me earlier?" She looked at the woman that he was, the high-heeled woman. "You know her?"

"She's the woman I was telling you about earlier. Her car, he pushed it into the traffic and caused all of this mess." Boyd asked if she was in trouble. "Only in the sense that this guy is out for her ass. As I said before, lucky for her she wasn't in the car when he hit it from the rear end. There is footage, too, of him being abusive to her when she left work. Or tried to.

31

She's a nice woman—Colin liked her right off."

He couldn't fathom having someone think it was all right to shove another person into traffic like this man had. Nor to have such a hatred for someone that you'd even think of doing that. When the woman leaned against the nurses' station and kicked her shoe off, he thought it was the sexiest thing he'd ever seen when she started curling and uncurling her toes along her calf.

Before he could think that it was a bad idea or even a good one, he found himself walking toward her. When one of the nurses smiled at him, the woman turned and looked at him. It was the first time Boyd had seen her face, and he was blown away by the sheer loveliness of her.

"Miss Pratt, this is Boyd McCullough. Doctor Boyd, this is Reilly Pratt. You and Miss Mac operated on her daddy."

He might have thanked the nurse, but he couldn't think beyond Reilly's beauty. He knew he was staring, but just couldn't help himself. So, when she turned to look around, no doubt to escape the loony that he was acting like, he took her hand into his before he spoke. The shock of their touching had him moaning and then holding onto the nurses' station as well.

"Are you all right?" He nodded but didn't let go. "You've been working really hard, maybe you need to sit down for a minute. Let me see if there's someone that can help you."

When Reilly started to walk away, he grabbed her again. "No. No, please. I'm all right. As you said, just tired. If you would just sit with me for a few minutes, I'll tell you how your dad is doing."

Boyd didn't have any idea why he was feeling

overwhelmed by the woman. Yes, she was very beautiful, and she smelled like fresh lemons. But he'd seen beautiful women before. An odd thing to think someone smelled like, but he was sure that's what he was smelling. He asked her about it when they were seated in the nurses' station behind the desk.

"The hand sanitizer has a lemony smell to it. I think it smells really good too. Like lemon pie or tarts." He sniffed her again when she put out her hand to him. "I didn't have any idea what to do to help. I'm afraid I faint at the sight of blood, so I think they made me busy work. But it was nice to be able to help some of these people. After all, I was sort of some of the cause, I guess."

"No, Lauren is saying that you were simply lucky that you were out of the car. But as for the names and numbers, it will go a long way in contacting family when we find things after this is all done. Sometimes it's a bag of clothing or a watch. Most of the time we just use the list to call the family back to see if they needed any more assistance." He smiled at her, feeling well out of his territory right now. "About your dad. He's going to be fine once he starts to heal better. He took a nasty fall, and had we not been there, I shudder to think what would have happened to him. But we have him sedated so he won't be moving around too much. Healing quietly, after so much trauma, is the best thing for him."

Boyd told her of his injuries and what they'd done to fix them. Also of his broken arm, as well as all the other places that he'd stitched him together. He told her that he was in good health and that would work in his favor a great deal. He could see the relief on her face, and was glad that he'd been able to do that for her.

"I've recently moved in with him. For financial reasons. Anyway, he wasn't taking his medication regularly, so I started to keep an eye on them for him. And his diet. He's lost a few pounds and is exercising now as well. He's sort of forgetful when he's working, and I just gently remind him of them." Boyd told her that was all good. "He's all I have in the world right now. And he's been supporting me for a while. I've run into some issues that he's helping me out of."

It was on the tip of his tongue to tell her that he'd help her too, but he just managed to catch himself. Boyd wasn't sure what was going on right now, but he wanted to hold her hand and not let her go. When Colin came to talk to him, he found his cat all pissy about him and growled low.

"I just need to ask her a question, Boyd. I won't touch her." Reilly looked at him oddly, but he wasn't having it. "Boyd, are you all right?"

"I don't know." And he didn't either. Looking at Reilly, who was still staring at him, he told her he was sorry. "I have to check on some patients and then go home. Yes, I should go home. It's quiet there, so I can think. And I think I need a nap as well."

He left them standing there and hurried to his car. By the time he was home, he was so jittery that he wondered if he should have been driving. Going into his little condo, he dropped his keys on the floor and fell, fully clothed, onto his bed. He'd nap, then go back. Boyd told himself he'd feel better after a nap.

Chapter 3

Rich pounded on the door again. He was worried about his boy. When he'd not answered his phone nor his calls to him through their link, he made his way to his house to find out what happened. Just as he was ready to bust in the door, it finally opened. Not waiting for an invite in, Rich shoved his way past his son and into his tiny place.

"How on earth can you live like this? There isn't enough room in here to swing a pup. Not without knocking everything off to the floor." Boyd grumbled something about pups, but he didn't rightly understand him. "You going to come out of this cave and come out with the living?"

"I was exhausted." His dad told him that a lot of people were. "Yes, well, I was just taking a little nap. Until someone had to come and bust in the door and wake me."

"A nap? Heck fire boy, you've been here for two days. Nary a peep out of you, either. I was worried sick about you. That's the reason I came here today." He asked him if he was

35

sure about the days. "Of course I'm sure. I know what day of the week it is. And that accident out there on seventy-five, it was two days ago too. You go on and take a shower and I'll talk to your mom. You're lucky that she didn't come here with me. She'd have been none too happy with you right now."

When Boyd went to take his shower, Rich told Bea what Boyd had told him. And how he'd not had a clue it had been so long. She asked him what they were going to do now.

I got him to take himself a shower. He didn't stink too bad, but I thought it would go a long way in waking him up. Then I'll bring him home to you. She asked if he'd spoken to him about his mate. *I just told you what I said to him. Did you hear me mention about a mate? No. And you want to know why? Because I didn't mention it yet.*

Richard McCullough, you speak to me that way again and I'll show you what a mate can do to her other half. I've been worried about him too, so don't be saying that's what has you snapping at the woman who does your laundry. He almost pointed out that she didn't do it either, but thought he might live longer if he didn't. *Now, I want you to wait before talking to him about her. I want to be there when you do.*

He told her that he was sorry, he had been worried about him. She asked him nicely to bring Boyd home to her and she might forgive him. Rich made himself a mental note to stop and get her some pretty flowers on the way home too. He didn't like her upset with him any more than he liked being upset with her.

Rich wondered about the girl himself. She was a pretty little thing, and he was happy to see that her daddy was mending pretty well too. Of course, there was no reason to think that he wouldn't, in Rich's mind. He had the best of the best working on him. But making Boyd see that she was his mate, that was going to take some talking. He, like Colin, didn't think that Boyd had understood what he'd been doing that day.

As soon as Boyd had his shower and was dressed, they headed to the flower shop. He knew it wasn't called that, but in the last few months, the place had changed its name twice. He couldn't have remembered it if someone had paid him to tell them. Boyd went in with him.

"You getting someone some pretty flowers too?" He said he was getting them for his mom, he'd worried her. "You worried me too. But I don't want no flowers. How about you get me a soda pop? One of the cream sodas like I like."

"Dad, I thought Mom said that you were cutting back on sweets." Rich wanted to tell him to let him worry about his mom, but he was buying her flowers because he'd messed up, and he didn't think that would get him in good with his son right now. "I'll get you one, but if Mom smells it on your breath, I'm going to plead the fifth."

"You do that." He got Bea two dozen yellow and pink roses. It was close to Christmas, but he didn't want her thinking of that particular day when he gave them to her. That's why he didn't get the pretty red ones with the greenery in them. As they were put into a pretty bow, he watched as Boyd bought himself one of the newspapers.

"You missed a lot of stuff going on with that accident. The guy that caused it all, he's saying that he had nothing to do with it, and that it's all that little girl's fault." He asked what little girl. "The one whose daddy is in the hospital. You operated on him."

Rich knew that he was talking a little loud, so he calmed himself down. Boyd asked him if he was all right, and he told him that he had a lot on his mind. He looked at the flowers when they were handed to him and cocked a brow at him.

"Don't you go making snap judgments on me. I messed up, but I'm making up for it, ain't I?" Boyd said nothing as he asked for a dozen red roses. "I've been worried about you, that's all, and it has me a little on edge."

"I'd say you're a lot on edge, and that it hasn't much to do with me sleeping for so long. Why don't you tell me why it is you came to get me? The real reason, Dad, not the one that you told me you came by for." He told his son that he didn't know what he was talking about. "Sure you don't. When you have something on your mind, like you do right now, and you can't tell anyone about it, you get testy."

"I do not." Boyd pointed out the few times that he'd had a secret and how mean he'd been when he couldn't tell anyone. "This is different. Your mom, she wants to be there when you're talked to about this here thing."

"This here thing is about what?" Rich was going to crack under the pressure or he was going to lose his temper. Either way, he'd be in Dutch with the wife. "Dad? What is this about?"

"You and your mate." Boyd thanked the lady and took his flowers out to the car. He had the engine running by the time Rich made his own way out and sat in the passenger side of his own car. "I can drive, you know."

"I don't have a mate, Dad. I told you why the other day." Rich told him he knew what he'd told them. "Then you know that my mate and my chance of having a full life with her is not going to happen. I don't know what you think, but you're wrong."

The rest of the trip was made in silence. But he told Bea what had happened. How he'd been tricked. She huffed at him and told him he was too easy.

Easy? I do not think that I'm easy. He pressured me, just like I told you. And he is all upset with me now too. She asked him if he and Boyd were still coming over. *Yes. I got him in my car. He's driving though. So I can't rightly say if we'll make it there or not. I think that Colin has it about right. He don't understand.*

I'm thinking that you both might be right about it. If you thought that it was over, a done deal as you're so fond of saying, then you'd be inclined to think the same thing. Don't you agree? He said that he thought he would. *See? Once we get him here, now that he knows about the reason, I'll not have to beat around the bush so many times before I can bring her up. By the way, the poor girl is without a car or anything to get her around in. I was thinking that I'd lend her my car until Boyd can get her one she can use. What do you think of that idea?*

He told her what he always said when she had an idea. *You know what's best. And if she don't want to drive that around, I'll make sure that she has something in her driveway. Where is she staying anyway?*

The hospital. The poor thing won't leave there with her dad so ill. He was cut up pretty badly, from what I've been told. Rich knew that as well. And then the accident occurred and that had taken a great deal out of a lot of people. *I'll just pop over and see her sometime today. Maybe she'll let me sit with him while she goes and gets herself something to eat or some fresh air.*

39

We're about home. I think he's a mite upset with me, just so you know. And he might be with you too once you start talking to him. She said that she figured that already. *Also, I'm terribly sorry. I've had it pointed out to me that I'm a little mean when I have something I need to hold close to my vest. I'm right sorry about that, love.*

I love you, you old poop. Now get here so we can tell our son that he's not without love in his life.

For some reason he thought it was going to be harder to convince Boyd of that than it was for Lauren to not kick some butt when she was interrogating someone. He laughed at what he'd thought and wondered if Lauren would think it was funny too. She was very intense when she was.... Well, heck fire. She was always intense.

He looked out the window of the car as they drove. Rich had to admit that he loved this time of year. The crunch of the snow under his boots when he was out. The crisp breezes that blew up from the fields, reminding him that there was still life yet in the ground and trees. Watching the few horses that they still had on the ranch made him smile, and he loved to watch them frolic a little by throwing up the snow with their nose. As soon as they were home, he got out and took a deep breath of the fine weather. Snow always smelled fresh to him.

When Boyd passed him for the house, he wondered when the last time was that Boyd had looked around. Had let his animal out to play. He'd bet his last nickel that it had been a while. The boy worked hard all the time, and he wondered if he was making up for not having a mate. Or, missing the one that he'd had. Either way, his world was about to get turned right upside down, and Rich was going to enjoy it.

Laughing, he made his way to the house, wondering what the new year would bring. Then he stopped in his tracks. His mind went to his next mate-able son, Hawkins was next. And the mate that he had coming, she'd have to be gentle with his boy. Not just gentle, but strong as an ox too. Hawkins wasn't going to be an easy person to love, he had a feeling. He was hard, and full of something that made him what he'd been for the Army.

Going in the house, he thought about talking to his son. Asking him, just on the sly like, what he was thinking about when it came to his mate. He was almost afraid to do that. Like Lauren, Hawkins could be a mite on the intense side when he was upset. Probably all the time, really. But he'd talk to him. Soon.

Bea was fussing over the flowers that Boyd got her when Rich entered the house. He handed her his and she cried. Something else about women that he didn't understand. They cried when they were happy and when they were sad. Sometimes he wasn't sure what sort of piddle he'd get himself into when she did it. But he hugged her and told her that he loved her with either kind of tears, and that made her happy too.

Rich thought that he might not know women at all. They confused him and set his temper on high at times. But he knew they loved to be loved and cherished. And Rich had learned over his lifetime how to cherish and love like no other. And he did love his wife with his entire being.

~~~

Reilly held her dad's hand and told him all what she'd been up to. She did avoid the topic of Ross and the horrific accident, but she thought about it a great deal. When she saw something on the news or heard people talking about it, she would shiver about how close she'd come to dying out there that day. Not to mention, Lauren had come by to see her with Joe, and they had told her that she wasn't being arrested but she wasn't to leave town. She explained to them that with her father here, she had nowhere left to go.

"We've arrested Ross. I'm telling you that so that you'll at least feel marginally safer while you're out and about. I've yet to talk to his family face to face just yet, so there is that as well. Mr. Dander is a good man from all accounts, but something is wrong with his son. A lot is wrong with him." Reilly asked Joe if he was going to see him soon. "Yes. But you have nothing to worry about. The recording that you had in your car has established that he rammed you from behind. Also that you exited your car long before it was in the accident. Lauren was able to get someone to work on the recording and it turned out just fine. As well as the other phones we were able to have a look at besides yours."

"I've never seen him like that before. I mean, he was sexually harassing me at work, but never was he ever violent to me." Joe said that sometimes a person just snaps. "Yes, well, if it's all the same to you, I'm not going to leave here without an escort. He fucking scared me. And to have hurt all those people for no other reason than he didn't want me to quit working so I could come here just scares me to the point where I think I might need a bodyguard too. You have no idea what it was like to see him doing that to me. And to have thought it was funny."

"I'm sure that it was more than that. I'd probably go so

far as to say that it might not have had a thing to do with you. You just happened to be in that place when it came to a head. But you're right, I'd not leave here unless someone goes with you." She assured them that she had no intentions of that. "Also, I know that you've meet Dustin when he came to stay with you yesterday, so if you do want to leave, I'll send him to be with you for the time being.

Now she sat by her father's bedside, waiting for him to wake up so that she could tell him what had happened to her. And that she loved him so much. Reilly knew that they were keeping him a little doped up, just so he'd not be in too much pain, but she still worried for him. He really was all that she had in this world.

Watching the news when it came on again, she wasn't surprised when they showed footage from the wreck on the highway. Her car, she could see it now, really had been the instrument of death for a lot of people. Even seeing the big semis trying to come to a stop but flipping to their side, slowly falling over onto two cars, had her cringing with each second of it. She was able, too, to see it from different angles from the cell phones that had been recording it. It didn't lessen her car's involvement in the entire thing. Then they showed her footage from the hill where she'd gotten out to be sick.

It was of the car, Ross's car, when he had pushed her car onto the road. Him just sitting there, smoke coming from not just the rear of his car but the front end too where he had hit her. When he finally got out of the car, she could see when he turned to look in her direction and wondered if he'd seen her there what he would have done. But he danced. A dance of pure joy at what she could only assume was his entertainment of what was happening before him.

When the news reporter spoke, Reilly read what it said below the reporter's picture. The sound had been turned off so as not to disturb her dad. But she showed how they had blown up the picture of the man there, and there was no mistaking that it was Ross Dander. None at all. And she told how he'd been arrested as well.

The nurse came in a few minutes after she turned off the television and asked her if she needed anything. Telling her no, she was fine, she decided to go down to the cafeteria and have some dinner. It was the only place that she could get to without a car. The nurse said that she'd keep an eye on her dad for her and let her know if there were any changes.

Reilly had no money. No cards either. Her purse was a part of the evidence that was used in the mass accident, along with her cell phone and other things that were in the car. They had given her dad's things to her, or she'd have no money to eat on. Lucky for her, he had about two hundred dollars in his wallet or she'd be starved about now. Going up to eat, she rode the elevator with a nice older man and his wife. They were going to see their first great-great-grandchild.

The cafeteria was never full, which she didn't understand. The food was really good, they served it on real plates, and cloth napkins were at each of the tables. Today she had a roast turkey dinner with all the trimmings, and a glass of the best tea that she'd ever drank. As she was cutting up her turkey, someone sat down beside her. She knew the face—he looked a great deal like his brothers.

"I'm Hawkins. I go by Hawk." She nodded. "I'm also one of the McCullough brothers. I've been sent to bring you to my parents' house for dinner."

"As you can see, I'm already eating." He took her plate from her and took it to the elderly man sitting in the corner with a coffee. When he thanked him for the meal, Hawk pointed to her. The man tipped his imaginary hat at her and dug into her meal. She looked at Hawk when he sat back down. "I was going to eat that."

"Yes, well, now you can come with me." Reilly didn't want to be charmed by him, but for some reason she was. "You're looking at me like I'm a speck on your blouse that you don't want. I'm a nice man."

"Yes, I think you are. But you're very misunderstood too, I'm thinking. You want people to be afraid of you, but you're nothing but a puppy, aren't you?" For an answer, he laid a gun, knife, and a long piece of wire on the table before he put his hand over all of it and shifted his hand into a long blade. "Are you trying to impress me or scare me?"

"Both. Are you coming with me nicely? Or do you want me to carry you out on my back? I'm up for either." She stared at him. "Don't analyze me please. You might be right on some of it, and then I'd have to prove to you that you aren't even close to the mark."

"I was told not to leave here unless I had an escort. Who would have sent you?" He nodded and told her that Lauren did. "Who else would know that I'm here?"

"My entire family. If you don't come with me, I'm going to tell you that they'll come here. All of them. With babies and in-laws and all the things that come with having children en masse. They're an overload that you don't want to bring to the hospital, I swear." She asked him why they had invited her in the first place. "I was told to come and get you for dinner. Other than that, I don't have any idea. You'll learn, when my mom tells you to do something, you do it and don't ask too many questions."

"You're afraid of your mom." He told her that they all were. "Just how many people are there coming here, if I don't go with you?"

"Thirty? I don't know, really. I have six brothers. Four of them are married with children. My parents will come of course, and in-laws of the wives will come along. Just to annoy you." She told him she didn't annoy easily. "I do. And I will if you don't come with me. I really am able and willing to protect you."

She stood up with him. "Do you think I need protecting? Last I heard, Ross was in jail for murder and for attempted murder. I thought I was safe from him."

"Not his father if he should get it in his head that you put his son there. If it were me, I'd be happy someone did it. But that's just me." He took her to the main floor by the elevator, and then out to a monster truck that was sitting right in front. There were "no parking" signs everywhere, but obviously he didn't heed them. Getting into the truck with his help, Reilly was surprised by the sheer amount of electrical equipment that was on the dashboard and seat. It was like he was doing missile launches from his truck.

He didn't say anything more on the drive to his parents' house, but she needed a few answers. Hawk had shifted his hand into a lethal weapon. He carried around enough weapons to win a small skirmish. She looked at him as he turned onto the main street of the town that she had only just moved to.

"You're sort of Army, aren't you?" He nodded and said something like that. "I see. And this show of weapons, I'm assuming that you're a shifter of some kind. Elite, I think is what you'd be called."

"No, not an elite, but something more." Hawk glanced at her as he drove. "I was dying, and my nephew gave me a bit of his blood so that I'd be healed. It also made me a true immortal. We all are, as a matter of fact."

"Are all your family members the same? I mean, the more part of being a shifter?" He told her that some were, others were not. But he said they were usually just jaguars. He asked her who she had known that was a shifter. "One of the men that I worked with. He was a wolf. His family has been around here for a long time, I guess."

"The local pack is a friend of my family as well. They help us when we need it, and we do the same for them. It's a nice way to keep poachers out of our lives, and people who have no business being on our property where they might be doing things to hurt either of us." She nodded and looked out the window. "Did he ever explain to you about mates? Did he have one?"

"Yes. He and his mate have been together for a long time. Years and years. They have several children too." Hawk nodded. "Why do you ask? I'm not your mate, am I?"

"No, but you could be one of my brothers'. Boyd." She asked if that was the doctor. "Yes, that's him. He had one, a very long time ago, and she was killed in an accident. We've always been told that we have one shot at having a mate, but my mom has some information that says that sometimes, once in a great while, another might come into our lives."

"So, you're taking me there for some kind of test or something?" He told her it was more like a test for Boyd rather than her. "Are you offering me up as some kind of special prize if I am? Is that what this invitation is all about? I'm to be mated to a man I don't know or care to know? If that's it, you can take me right back to the hospital right now. I'm not going to be anyone's mate, if that's what this is about."

"Don't get your head all twisted up. I'm just having a conversation with you about it. You asked and I'm telling you. But if you aren't Boyd's mate, then what are you out? Nothing but a bit of your time, and you get to have a fantastic meal that will fill your belly more than the hospital food will." She asked what would happen if she was. "Then you have an entire family that will be there for you. Love you like you've never been loved before, and the support of so many people that you'd never have to worry again. We're here."

She looked at the house in front of her. It was massive and old. She'd bet anything that it had been in the family for more generations that she could count on one hand. There were rockers on the wraparound porch, as well as empty planters that she'd bet were filled to overflowing in the summer. Right now, they held Christmas decorations in them, as well as lights around each window, which also had a candle glowing in them.

"They know that you told me, I'm betting." Hawk said that he had told them, yes. "What do they expect of me, Hawk? I'm not a person that has anything. I've had to give up everything for personal reasons, and that left me without a great deal of even personal things. I live with my dad because

I don't have anywhere else to go. I only have a car — well, had a car — because he gave me my mom's old one. I don't come from this kind of grandeur."

"Few do, I would guess. My family has had money from the very start, I think. We do as well, all of us do. Thanks a great deal to our brother, who invests well for us and sells when it's better. My parents taught us the meaning of money and what it could do for us, as well as how it could harm us. And it does a great many people." Reilly nodded. "But sitting here is not going to give you any more than you want to take. My brother, if you are his mate, is the kindest, most gentle person you'll meet. But he's also protective and smart. You couldn't do any better. But you won't find out what you have or not until you get out of the car and go up there."

A man came outside on the porch and leaned against the long column that was a part of the porch. He didn't come to her, for which she was glad when she figured out it was Boyd, but waited on her. When the door on the driver's side opened, then closed, she watched Hawk go to Boyd and pat him on the shoulder before he went into the house. Boyd moved then, coming to the truck and getting in on the driver's side.

She turned to look at him when he started the truck up and moved out of the drive. Wherever she was going with him, she hoped that he knew how to drive this monster. To be honest, she was a little afraid of it.

49

Chapter 4

Boyd drove to the house that her dad had had his accident in. As they drove along, he thought about the fact that she might be his mate. He tried not to think about it as he drove, but his mind kept going to when she had stretched her toes when her feet were tired.

"This house that we're going to see, it's the one that your dad fell at. It's since been repaired, but it's on the market and I thought we'd go and see it before we had dinner." She didn't say anything, and he tried to fill the quiet space with something. "He's doing really well, by the way, and tomorrow when I go see him, I'll take him off the morphine and wake him up a little more. He shouldn't be in nearly as much pain, but he will have some."

"Why are you taking me to see this house? Have you discovered that I'm your mate, or are you hoping to get laid?" He nearly drove off the road and had to steady his hands. "I'm not easy, as you'll find out. And whether or not I'm your mate doesn't mean shit to me. I've discovered that having a man in my life isn't all that much fun. They can be, I guess, but I don't have the time for one. So whatever your plans are for me, you'd better be rethinking them right now."

"I have no plans other than to get myself a house. And since you didn't seem to want to meet my family—which I have to say is probably a smart move on your part because they're invasive and nosey. Pushy too when they think that they're right. I thought it would be better if you went house-hunting with me. Hawk said that you don't have much, and that's fine too." She asked if they were mates or not. "I don't know. I would have to get closer to you to smell your throat. That's the only sure tell sign that I know of."

They stopped in front of the house and he took the papers that Lauren had given him on the house. As Reilly looked them over, he stared at the house. He liked it all right, he supposed. He also thought it was big.

"It has five bedrooms on the second floor and a master suite on the third. There is also an elevator in the back of the house somewhere, as well as a couple of dumbwaiters. The right side of the house has a screened in porch that has glass panels that can be used in the winter months. They're not in right now—something about the house being closed up for the sellers. The left side of the house is the kitchen, laundry, as well as a good-sized pantry. My dad said that when they put it in about four years ago, it was state of the art. He doesn't know what the kitchen looks like now, but he didn't do the work on it." She opened the door and got out. Boyd laughed when she turned and glared at him from the snow-covered sidewalk. Getting out, he helped her over the worst of the snowbanks and opened the door with the key he had from earlier. He continued telling her what he'd read about the house. "It has very little in the way of improvements since it's been shut up. The heat is on, but the water has been turned off. Until it sells."

As soon as they were in the door, he looked up to the banister and saw that it wasn't fixed, but the blood and wood had been cleaned up since he'd been there before. She walked to the stairs and looked up without going anywhere. Then she turned to him.

"This sniffing thing you have to do. Is that all there is to it? You just have to sniff me?" He nodded, unsure where she was going but hoping for the best. "You touch me other than absolutely necessary, and I'll make you regret it, understand?"

"Yes." He moved toward her slowly, thinking that if she wasn't his mate, he'd take her out. She was beautiful and strong. Sexy too. "If you'd remove your scarf and tilt your head, I'll not have to touch you to find out. But you might feel something too. Reese, Dustin's wife, said that it could make you slightly dizzy when your body realizes it for what we are to each other."

When she removed her scarf, he noticed a scar there. He wanted to ask about it, but it was really none of his business, so he didn't. What it did, however, was make him want to feel her skin, smell her heat. Touch his fingers to her throat to see if he could feel if it was as soft as it looked. Instead, he just buried his nose as close to her skin as he could and inhaled deeply of the scent that was all hers.

"Christ."

Boyd thought that she had that about right. He held her

53

then when she staggered slightly. Not like he wanted to—Boyd wanted to pull her to his body and take her right then. But he also knew that if he moved too fast or manhandled her in any way, she'd be pissed off, and so would his family at him. Instead, he pulled back and let her go when she seemed steady on her feet.

"Are you all right?" She nodded, then shook her head. "Yes, I'm right there with you on that. I'm sorry. I had no idea. If you didn't understand, that was a positive test."

"So, we're mates." He nodded at her statement and tried to wrap his mind around having a mate. "I don't know how I feel about that. Overwhelmed for sure. And slightly terrified of what comes next."

"Nothing will come next unless you want it to. I mean, I want you, right now, but I know that we barely know each other, and we have time." She nodded and looked around the floor they were on. "I do need a house for us, if or when you want to make this move. This one has a lot of features that I like, some I don't care about. Others...well, there is a lot to be said for a house this old and well maintained."

"I had a two-bedroom apartment a while back. It wasn't really as large as that might sound. Saying that it had two was really overstating the actual size of the rooms. I had my bed in one of the rooms, and my dresser and other things in the other one." She moved through the doorway into what he thought could be a living room. "The fireplace is very nice in here. I can see a massive fire in here on cold nights."

"My parents have one as well. But when we started leaving home, they had a gas one put in. Chopping wood for a fire was too much work, my dad told us, and he just liked to have a nice fire when it was just the two of them." She smiled at him, and Boyd wanted to see her do that more. Just smile at him. "I think the dining room is just past this room."

They explored the whole house. It was going to need a great deal of work. And when they were in the front hall again, he asked her what she thought of the house. He really didn't care for it as a whole.

"It's all right. It wouldn't be my choice if I could have any that I wanted. The kitchen is really small, don't you think, for a house this large?" He told her that even if you added in the pantry, it was very small. "And the back yard is sort of a disappointment too. I mean, I would imagine that you'd need room to run, but I don't think you'd get very far without running into that large stone wall there."

"I hadn't even noticed that until you mentioned it upstairs. And I have to be honest with you, I'm not all that thrilled about having to come down three flights of stairs in the morning when I get up." They both laughed. The elevator was there but it didn't work, and he'd bet that it would take a great deal of time and effort to get it going again. "I would like to have children someday if possible. If so, then I'd like to be on the same floor as them."

"You want children then?" He told her he did, but it would be her body, so she would be the one to decide if and when they had them. "Just like that? You'd let me tell you that we aren't having children, and you'd be all right with it?"

"As I said, it's your body. The one that would have the most pain and suffering with having children. As a doctor, I see firsthand what having a child can do for and to a woman. No, I'd have no say, I wouldn't make anyone do something

55

like that if they didn't want to." She nodded and looked at the front door. "Do you want them?"

"Yes. A lot of them, as a matter of fact. I'm an only child of two parents that were only children. I like people a great deal. Right now, I'm terrified of them, and with good reason, but I'm usually happiest when I can be around them." She smiled at him. "I've met a couple of your brothers, and I can only assume that they're all big like you are. That's a little much to be around, even for a person that loves to be with people."

"Yes, we're all large men. My dad is as well." She nodded. "My mom is this tiny little stick of dynamite that is so sweet until she feels that she's been taken advantage of, or someone is hurting her baby boys. She still calls us all that. Her boys."

"My dad calls me his little peanut. It's embarrassing a little, but I love him very much." He told her it showed. "Do you have any more to look at? Houses, I mean. I have to get something to eat soon, however. Hawk gave my meal at the hospital to a very thankful man tonight."

"I'm sorry. I didn't think. I've been.... Well, having a mate can really distract a man. And with all this other stuff going on, it's been a really hard few days even for me." Boyd helped her out to the truck again, asking her what she wanted to eat. "There are only a few choices to have around here. Or we can go back to my parents' house and have leftovers. I'll find out first if there are any."

"I'd rather just get to know you, if that's all right for now." He said it was and asked her how she liked pizza. "Sounds wonderful. Do you know if they serve iced tea? The unsweet kind? I can't stand soft drinks, and sweet tea makes me ill."

"A woman after my own heart. Yes, they have amazing

tea. And the best garlic bread I've ever eaten too." As he drove them over, careful of the snowdrifts on the road, he told her about the other houses. "Lauren has decided that I need to have a larger house. I have a condo now, but I'm actually not there much. Mom has us over once a week, and then I'm usually eating in town when I'm working. It's just been easier not to have to worry about cutting grass and all the stuff that goes along with having your own home."

"My dad loves to cut grass. He could have done it daily if the grass would have done him a favor and grown enough so that he could." They both laughed as they entered the restaurant. She talked about her dad like he did his, with wonderment and exasperation too. "He does this thing for owners now. It's sort of like he's this ringer for them. He goes to open houses for them, finds out what he can from the realtor, then has me do the research on the place. It's been fun for us both."

"My brother just bought a house recently. It was owned by this wealthy older woman who had a sister. And when the homeowner passed away, her sister moved in and had her entire life boxed up and put in the barns there. All of it was nicely packaged and none of it was ruined, but Larson and Virginia are having so much fun going through it all and putting some of the pieces in their home. Dad is finishing up on that one now." She said that sounded like something she'd like to do too. "You should go over there sometime. He'd love the help, and I know that Virginia would. They've just gotten married and adopted her nephew as their own. Poor little fella had a rough start to his little life, but he's doing much better now."

They talked about everything and anything. When they were finished, Boyd didn't think anything of her going with him on the rest of the house searches. They decided that the next one they looked at was too chopped up. The dining room was on the other side of the house away from the kitchen. And there were no fireplaces. It seemed they both wanted that. Talking about their likes and dislikes, it was easier for them to look at what was on the list and cross out the ones that didn't suit them.

Then they started looking at the houses that Lauren deemed too far away or in the wrong place. Whatever her reasons were, they drove to one home that he knew was much closer to his family than even Hawkins' was. They pulled into the drive, and neither of them moved for several minutes.

"If this place has a fireplace, I want it." Reilly said they'd not be that lucky. "I tell you what, if we like it, we can have a fireplace put in later. Deal?"

"Yes, deal. Oh my, I'm almost afraid to go and see it. It's so perfect from this view. Look at the porch, Boyd. It's almost like your parents' but for the long windows on this one." They got out just as someone was coming out of the house. The woman said they could come on in, she was only getting her mail. They met in the front hall and even from there, the huge fireplace was visible. Just one more thing to tick off their list. It needed to have a huge library.

"Hello." Mrs. Winston introduced herself to them and asked if they were looking for a home. "Yes. We've just started our search today, as a matter of fact."

"Well, this one has been on the market for a little while. I think it's because we want to sell it as it sits. You see, it

belonged to my mother, and when she passed away several
months ago, none of us wanted to go to the trouble of selling
off her things. I mean, all her personal things are gone, but
the furniture and such, that comes with it. After someone
purchases it, they can deal with it." He asked her why they'd
do it that way and not call someone to come in and take the
furniture off their hands. "There are four of us children left
of Mom and Dad's. There aren't any fights about what we
wanted or not, but the will stipulates that we do it this way.
Each of us got to take what we wanted, but honestly, we've all
been around the block a few times and didn't need anything.
Her clothing was donated to the local clothing bank to use.
The food too that she didn't use. Mom was in her nineties,
so she had collected a great many things, and she thought
that her tastes should reflect in this home. I'm not sure if her
attorney had tried to talk her out of it or not, but this is what
we were left with. I loved my mom to pieces, but she could be
a pain in the butt. So, you two have yourself a look around. If
you have any questions, each of the rooms has a button near
the light switch that will relay to the kitchen what you have to
say. The intercom system was put in when my parents were
very young and having children. It still works wonderfully,
too."

Boyd wanted it to have a library in the worst kind of way.
But they took their time and started their looking about in
the kitchen. It was as spacious as any he'd seen in any of his
family's homes, and more up-to-date too. He was going to be
hard pressed to not buy this house. He hoped that Reilly liked
it as much as he did right now.

~~~

Joseph Dander hated coming to the police station to talk to his son. If it had been left up to him, he'd have washed his hands of him years ago. As it was, he was forever dealing with some kind of scam or even trouble that he got in yearly. But this last several months had been the worst.

There wasn't anything that was huge that Ross got into. Mostly stuff like shoplifting from a local store. A fender bender that was considered a hit and run had cost him. And lately there had been an escalation to his trouble that scared Joseph more than just a little.

As soon as he was seated in the little area where the phones were, he looked around as he waited for Ross to come. The place was spit clean, and there didn't seem to be anything outdated in the way it was painted. He noticed things like that.

Paint jobs on government buildings. The way the furniture was either too soft, which wouldn't last long, or was too uncomfortable. That could set a person off in no time. He also looked for cracks in the pavement and windows, as well as peeled paint on the bars. He'd been a long-time attorney for the government, and they had taught him to be not just observant, but to pay attention to his surroundings. The latter had served him well over the decades.

When Ross was seated across from him, he looked like someone had taken a few potshots at him. His lip was swollen, as was his eye. His knuckles were bloodied too. He asked him when he finally picked up the phone if he needed anything.

"Yes, I'd like to get out of here. Barring that, I'd like to have some decent clothes, as well as a meal that's not served on a paper tray with plastic silverware. What are you going to do about that woman that caused all this?" He asked him what woman. "That girl that worked for you and me. Reilly Pratt. She is the one that ran off without doing her job, and she is the one that pissed me off enough that I had to go and do something stupid."

"From what I've seen and heard from the police, all she did was want to go to the hospital when her father had been hurt. You, in some kind of stupor that I can only think of as idiotic, not only tried to detain her when she finally said that she was quitting, but you chased her across town in your car to ram her into oncoming traffic, which killed a few people as well as hurt a great many more. What the hell were you thinking, Ross?" He told him that she had abandoned her job. "No, she was working, got a call from the hospital, and left. Or she tried to leave. What sort of place are you running over there that you'd detain a person when they have a family emergency?"

"I am behind on research for a couple of cases, and she is the best there is. You want it to be right when you go to court, don't you? Well, she's the one that makes you win. If she left, there would be a shitty job turned in and you'd fail at something." Joseph wasn't sure, but he thought that his son was now blaming this entire episode on him as well as the young girl. "Besides, she was at fault just as much as I was. It was her car, for Christ's sake. Why isn't she in here like I am?"

"Did you know that she wasn't in the car when you hit her from behind, driving her into the traffic?" He said that he'd not known that. "So, you thought perhaps she was in the car when you maliciously did that to her. Mashed her car from behind so that she'd end up in traffic, going the wrong way and killing people."

"See, Dad, even you agree this is partly her fault. I bet if you could swing it, you could get me off by saying that it was all her." Joseph just shook his head. "They're saying that I'm responsible for those people having an accident and getting hurt. How the hell is it my fault? No one saw me hitting her car. For all we know, she might have just been having a shitty day too and drove herself into that mess. Why don't you say that part and get me out of here? I have to do things to keep me sane, and if I'm in here, like I am, then I'm not going to be able to do anything I want."

"I just told you that she wasn't in the vehicle when it hit that traffic. And they have video of you having yourself a little dance when you saw the wreckage that happened when you, with your car, ran hers into it." Ross just waved him off, as if that wasn't important enough to even mention. "Did you know that people were killed in that mess? That cars were crushed under semis that couldn't stop in time? Do you remember looking at the cars piling up on each other in an effort not to slam into the car in front of them, thanks to you?"

"How is their driving any of my fault? They should have been going the speed limit. Or even paying attention to what was ahead of them. No, they're not blaming that on me. It's the truckers that did that part. And the people in the cars that weren't paying attention. That is not going to be blamed on me. I know the law too." He looked around as he continued. "Dad, please get me off of this. If you do, then I'll be the best son anyone has ever had."

"And how do you expect me to do that, Ross? You harassed her at work, grabbing her when she tried to leave. Hitting her car on the trunk when she was backing, carefully I might add, out of her parking space. They have you on video committing this heinous crime. There is footage of you ramming your car into hers, which continued on the same path until it caused traffic accidents that resulted in ten deaths, maybe more. As well as you dancing gleefully when cars began to pile up on each other at the accident itself. Some of those people were crushed when their cars were fallen upon by semis falling over on top of them." Ross was shaking his head no when he mentioned the semis again. "I don't know what to do with you, Ross. I surely don't. I can't believe, first of all, that you hurt that poor girl. It's all right there on her dashcam that she had on her car, recording the entire time you were with her. And you seemed disappointed when I told you that she wasn't in the car that you pushed."

"I am. I don't know if it was my intentions that she was to die, but you will admit it would have been easier on me had she been in the car when it was hit." He asked him why. "Then you could blame the entire thing on her and no one would be there to say anything differently. And I don't think she can record me with that thing in her car without my permission. You should get that thrown out of court. That'll help you some, don't you think? Dad, you have to do something. I have things that I really need to do to keep me sane. You have to do this for me."

Joseph didn't know what to say. He was sickened by what Ross was implying and saying. He'd wanted to kill that girl. What had she ever done to him, to anyone, that would cause so much hatred from him? Nothing in this world could he think of to have warranted such behavior. Standing up, he

63

told his son that he'd come by to see him perhaps tomorrow. But not to expect anything from him.

"You'll be here tomorrow? Good. And you'll see about a decent meal, right? And real silverware. If I have to stay here for much longer, Dad, I'm going to need some special treatment. I'm not cut out for jail. And don't try that shit that you've done before. I'm not going to jail for this for very long. You have to see it isn't my fault what happened out there. It's all on their shoulders, Reilly and the truckers. This isn't my fault at all." He just hung up the phone and turned his back on him.

He could have told him that no one was cut out for jail, that was the reason for it. And it should be hard on a person. Maybe that would keep them from coming back. But with his son, he knew that he'd only say it wasn't his fault, or again, blame it all on someone else. That poor girl. Joseph had done her wrong as well, he knew that now.

Joseph was tempted to just pretend that he didn't have a son. Just turn his back on him and not return. But he couldn't, not any more than he could have done it to his wife if she had needed him. He had his driver take him home. He needed to talk to Evelyn and perhaps take a long shower. Joseph felt dirty, like he'd been bathed in something nasty. Nasty words, that is. And all from a person that he'd helped create and had turned out to be a monster.

Evelyn was sitting in the sun room when he returned home. He knew that she'd been watching the news—there were spent tissues all around her lap, as well as tear stains on her cheeks. She had taken this very hard, harder than he had. He'd asked her not to do that, watch what people were saying about their son. But like him, she was hoping for some kind of miracle that would say that they had the wrong person. That their son hadn't committed these horrific crimes.

"He did this, didn't he, Joey? He killed all those people and now he's going to prison." She was the only person in the world who called him that. And he loved her for it. "Our son, who we tried our best to not ruin like others of our wealth did to their children, turned into a monstrous being. Someone that has no feelings for anyone but how things will affect him."

"Ross told me that he was disappointed that the young woman wasn't in the car when he hit her car into traffic. He told me that had she been killed like so many others had, then I could simply blame it all on her and no one would know the difference." Evelyn nodded and reached for his hand. He held it tightly in his own. "He wants me to get him off. Said he'd be the best son there ever was. And he wants a decent meal with real silverware."

"Oh Joey, what are we going to do? He's been so horrible his whole life, and even when we made him pay for his crimes, he never learned a lesson from any of it. He has no remorse at all for what he's done. But this, this is well beyond anything that he's ever done. He's never killed anyone, do you think?" Joseph said that he didn't know nor what they were to do. "You're not going to pay for him an attorney, for one thing. I don't think I could bring myself to know that we paid for this mess and he might get off because of us. Please, tell me that we won't do this."

"I won't, honey. I promise you that I won't hire anyone or do another thing for him." He'd not thought of the fact that he might get off, and was glad that she'd brought it up.

65

"I'm not going to go back there after tomorrow either. He's on his own. A grown man that has messed up badly and people were killed. I'm going to wash my hands of him. But I will—I'd like to go and tell this woman, Reilly Pratt, how very sorry I am that he's done this to her."

"If you'd not mind, I'd like to go with you if I can. My heart just breaks for what he's done to her. And we'll help her out anyway that she needs as well. I heard from one of the doctors at the hospital that her father was in a bad accident himself before this all came about." Joseph told her that he'd fallen through a banister. "That poor man. And Reilly. Yes, we'll help her out with his bills and such. Not a payoff, but something to tell her how sorry we are that this happened."

Sitting down at his desk a bit later, he looked up what he could find on the woman and her father. She had had some rough ways in the past, he could see. But instead of letting her dad—who could have afforded to help her pay off the debt that came to her—help her, she was making all the payments to the bank on her own, monthly and on time. He also found out that his son was correct on her being the best at the research firm that he used. Her name was on each of the reports that he'd used in court.

Even though he was retired now, Joseph did on occasion take a case or two. It kept him up on things. But most importantly, it got him out and moving about. He wasn't going to be one of the lawyers who late in their lives realized that they'd gotten lazy and fat while retired. Not him. He was going to go to his maker fit as a fiddle, if he could. Smiling at his own joke, Joseph made a call to a good friend of his, just to find out what he knew about all this with the young woman and what he could do to help her. Reilly was paying for a house that wasn't in her name, nor had it ever been. He wanted to know why.

Chapter 5

The house was absolutely perfect. And the way that the furniture seemed to call to him made him want to kick off his shoes and sit in the easy chair in the living room and enjoy a good book. And the library was magnificent.

It had oak shelves, long lines of books of every genre, old and new. He enjoyed looking at the titles as much as he did the rest of the room. The woman that had owned this home had an eclectic taste in books and things, just as he had his whole life. There was just too much to read for a person to pick one kind of books they liked.

"I would love to live here. Spend the rest of my days never leaving this house and being happy." Boyd told Reilly that he agreed with her. "I don't know what this place is going for, but if we can afford it, then I will do something to help with paying for it. I don't even care what it is."

She had said if *we* can afford it, and Boyd felt his heart fill at her words. They toured the rest of the house, finding that

69

the master bedroom was on the same floor as the others. There were plenty of bathrooms to accommodate the four bedrooms and large walk-in closets. Even the coverlets on the beds and the colors of the rooms were things that he might have picked out on his own.

"I think the kitchen is perfect, don't you?" Reilly said the house was. "Yes, well, of course it is. It's like the woman that lived here knew we were going to come here and see it."

He'd never been one that was mushy about things, but there were things in the house that reminded him of his parents' home. The comfort of it, too, was something that he enjoyed. As they made their way to the back yard, all he could do was stare at the large in-ground pool with a pool house. The boat house that was sitting out over the river that ran down the back of the land. He even loved that there were trees everywhere that were going to be spectacular in the spring and summer.

"Okay, I don't think I want to see anymore. Let's go and find out the price so that we can buy it. You think it's going to be expensive?" He told Reilly that he had no idea, but it would be worth it to ask. "All right. I'm too excited. You talk, and I'll be quiet. I don't want to mess it up by being too excited about this."

"I don't think I can be trusted not to beg her to sell it to us." He was having such a good time. And the fact that he was going to pay any price she wanted for the house, just to see Reilly this happy forever, only made him feel like he was getting the best deal for any price. "All right. I think I'm composed."

As soon as they walked into the kitchen where Mrs.

Winston was, they sat at the table with her. She just smiled at them, like she knew that they were going to make an offer. And Boyd did something that he'd never done before — he let his heart rule his mouth.

"We'll take it. No matter the price." When both her and Reilly laughed, he felt his face heat in embarrassment. But he wasn't upset with his blurt of words; in fact, he was happy to have been able to say it aloud. "Seriously, I don't know what the price is — we should have asked — but we love everything about the home. Including the library and fireplace, which is all we really talked about having."

"I need to tell you something before I tell you the price. My mother was a kind woman, generous to a fault. And she loved life and what she could get out of it more than she did working. To her, a day spent here at home with the things that she loved was a day well spent." Reilly told her that she thought it showed. "Yes, I think she would have liked you two very much. She was a wonderful woman, as I said, but she was also set in her ways, and now, with you two here, I can see the wisdom in her words. The house is yours for one dollar."

"I'm sorry, what did you say?" She repeated it to him with a large smile. "I don't understand. A dollar is very low, even if it wasn't fully furnished, it's very low. Don't you think so too?"

"Not to my mother it wasn't. In her will she said that she wanted us to put the house on the market, and to sell it to someone that would love the house, and the things in it, as much as she did. You said that you loved both. Nor did you ask how much we were selling it for." Reilly asked about what previous buyers were told. "Most people come here with the assumption that it's going to be well over their budget and that they want to haggle us down. We were told to do neither. When someone asked the price without saying how much they loved it, they were disqualified in buying it. If they haggled, they were again taken out of the ability to buy it. You did nothing but tell me you wanted the house, and as I said, you have decided to take the house and the contents, no questions asked. That was the sort of couple that she wanted to buy her home. Someone that would continue to make it what she'd started, and bring up children here that would, perhaps, someday do the same."

"This is just what we were looking for. It's perfect." Mrs. Winston said that she thought so as well. "But you have no desire to live here? With your mother's things?"

"No. I have some of her things that she gave to me, as do my brothers. And the house is much too large for someone my age anyway. I loved this house my entire life. When she stipulated in her will what she wanted done, we were so happy at what she had done, we took turns coming here to wait on people to come by and see it. Today, I knew it was going to be a perfect day because it would have been her birthday."

Boyd wasn't sure what to say, and when someone knocked at the back door, Mrs. Winston got up to let the person in. Boyd looked at Reilly, who was still looking unsure. He was as well. There had to be a catch or something. But when the gentleman introduced himself as Mr. Gable, the estate planner for Serenity Armstrong, he told them the same thing that Mrs. Winston had. The house was only one dollar, and that as soon as he paid, the deed would be turned over to him.

Even reading the paperwork, Boyd could see that the forms were cut and dried. It said that he bought the house as is, and that they would pay one dollar for the house. Asking if his brother could come and have a look at the contract, he was told that it was fine. Taking out his cell so as not to confuse the people with him, he asked Larson to come over to their new home and look over the contract. He said that he was nearby and would be there in less than five minutes. Boyd thought it was the longest five minutes of his life.

"This is perfectly legal." Boyd shook his head, thinking that this had to be wrong somehow when Larson finished reading it over. "It is. If you pay him, the deed and house will be yours. This tells you what the yearly taxes are and the land that comes with it. And before I got here, I had Lauren run a check on the house when you told me you were buying it, and according to her, there are fifty-five acres. And with the deed, it says that as well. You're getting one hell of a deal, and you should take it."

He didn't even have a dollar on him, and they all laughed when Reilly had to go out to the car and get her purse so that she could put her change with his. Together they managed to scrape up one dollar and eight cents. When he signed off on the deed with Reilly, so did Mr. Gable, and in less time than it took them to roam the house, they were homeowners.

When Mr. Gable left the paperwork with Larson to be filed, Mrs. Winston left as well. She gave them the keys to the house, some of the paperwork on the furnishings, as well as the combination to the large safe in the basement. It was a place that they'd not even looked at when they'd been looking around. Larson asked them how they'd managed to get a home like this for so cheap.

Reilly told him what they were told and how they were the only ones that had passed the test. When she got to the part about the library and the fireplace, Larson asked to be shown around. The house and all that was inside was theirs. Boyd was still having a hard time wrapping his mind around that. They were homeowners of a ready to move into home.

Showing him around the house, Boyd heard from Lauren. Not only did she find out that the will was correct in what was told to them, but it had been sitting on the market for sixteen months. He asked her what else she'd been able to find about the place.

There are no liens against the place. The taxes are all paid up until today. I'm assuming that they already contacted someone to have your name put on the records as owner too. And when I checked with the offices downtown, yours and Reilly's names were on pending paperwork as owners. As I told Larson, you have fifty-five acres, as well as a rental property in the back, but someone is living in the house that faces a street a couple of miles away. At any time you can ask them to move, but you have to give them six months' notice. If I were you, I'd leave them there. It's a nice income, and there has never been any issues with them as tenants. Boyd told her that he was having a hard time believing any of this. *Well, bucko, it's been your day for having what you thought impossible possible, huh? Anyway, I think you should know that the family knows that you bought a house and got yourself a mate, and are on their way to you as we speak. I didn't tell them, Larson did, damn it. I so wanted to be the one to do it.*

When his parents showed up, they had boxes of ornaments. He was so glad for them that he was leaving to get a tree when another vehicle filled with his family showed up. He and Reilly were apparently staying the night in their new home too, as someone had gone to his house to get an overnight bag, and had brought some of the things that Reilly had too. Just as he was getting his car out of the mess of cars of his family, Colin showed up with not only a large tree, but an outdoor blow up Santa for the yard. Before he knew it, they were ordering food to be brought to them and having a party.

Things were moving very fast, so fast that he had to find a place to just have quiet. Standing on the back deck, looking out over the yard, he thought of his day and wondered why his head hadn't exploded or something. Hawk came out of the woods in front of him and Boyd laughed.

"Do you ever do anything conventionally?" Hawk just grinned at him and sat down on one of the chairs that hadn't been covered in snow. Boyd sat in the other one, and was glad for Hawk being the quiet one in the family. "I have a house and a mate. Something that I never thought of having again."

"The house is nice. I knew Mrs. Armstrong when she was alive. I would come by when she called and sometimes when she didn't. A very nice woman, if a little on the daffy side." He asked him how daffy. "Not like crazy daffy. She was just living life to the fullest, and damn, she could really play a good game of chess with me."

"I'm overwhelmed." He said he could see that. "Hawk, that only leaves you now. How do you feel about that?"

He sat there quietly, and Boyd was in no rush to hear his answer. Hawk and he had been close at one time. Not that they weren't now, but when they were kids, Hawk had stood up for him when bullies would come around. And because Boyd was so smart, there were a lot of bullies when he'd been a kid.

"I suppose when she gets here, if she's out there, I'm going to make a fool of myself and be the mushy type." Boyd didn't laugh or comment. He wasn't sure if Hawk was kidding or not. "What am I going to do? I don't have any idea. But the way that my life has been going, I'd say that she's going to be one of those kinds of women that want to go shopping all the time. We'll have a frou-frou house that I'll hate, but I'll be so much in love with her that I won't care all that much."

"She might be just like you. Hard assed and militant." Hawk just smiled but said nothing more. "Reilly is my mate, and I know nothing about her. I suppose that I'll learn — we've plenty of time for that — but it's strange to me that this house came to us and we both love everything about it." Hawk told him that it happened like that sometimes, he supposed. "I guess."

"Reilly's in a spot of trouble. I know, so you know that Lauren does as well." He asked him if she was going to be hurt. "Not by the thing that she has going on in her personal life, but she's paying for a home that she doesn't own, nor did she ever live in it. I could tell you what happened, mostly how it really happened, but she should tell you."

"I can wait on her to tell me then. So long as it doesn't cause her any pain." He said that it was draining her financially. "I'll look into that then. Whatever it is, we can work something out."

"Good. She'll tell you, I'm sure, but let her, okay? Also, this thing with her boss. That isn't going to hurt her either, but it will Ross Dander. I've heard through the grapevine that his father, Joseph Dander, isn't paying for an attorney. He's washing his hands of him. From what I've heard, he should have done it long ago."

"I've heard only what the news is saying about this. And of course what Reilly has said. It doesn't sound to me like he's got a full basket of nuts in his head." Hawk said that was a good way to put it. "Do you know if she's going to be charged with anything? Last I heard Ross was telling everyone it was her fault."

"It wasn't, but that too is being looked into by Lauren and a couple of other people. It won't come down on her head at all, but she'll have to testify against him." He said she'd do that, he supposed. "Also, his father. Even if he has washed his hands of his son, Reilly filed a grievance against Ross several times and nothing was done about it. That will come back to bite Mr. Dander in the ass big time, I think. No one will be happy that he shoved this under the rug for so long."

They sat there for several more minutes, both of them, he thought, digesting what they knew. Boyd knew very little about his mate or her father, and less about what had happened that brought her to his life. He would have to have a long talk with her, but not right now. They were both enjoying that they'd done something together.

"Boyd, when I do find my mate, I was wondering if you'd be my best man when I get married." He was honored and touched by the question, and told him that. "Good. I thank you."

"Hawkins, knowing what I do about you, I'd like to ask you if you're happy with your life? Do you get up in the morning now and think you've made the right decisions about getting out of the service?" He didn't answer him right away, and Boyd didn't know if he would. But when he sat up in his chair, never looking at him, he was positive that he wouldn't. It wasn't until he opened his mouth that Boyd started seeing a side of Hawkins he'd never seen before.

~~~

Hawk had been having nightmares even before he'd left the service. Most of it was to do with what he'd done over there. The people that he'd killed or seen killed. The way he'd been used for things that were better left untold. He looked at his little brother, thinking that if he could just get a little bit of what he was feeling off his chest, he'd feel better. Hawk wasn't sure how Boyd would feel, but he would understand.

"When we were in country, we learned not to eat, drink, or touch things that we do here every day. The water, even in bottles, could be tainted with poison. The food rancid with worms and other things. And touching things would get you killed." Boyd nodded, and Hawk went on. "Once, when we were taking a break—and by break I mean that we were looking for our target while sitting around restaurants nursing bottles of beer that none of us touched. Anyway, we were sitting around waiting. When we were ordered where to go next, we gathered ourselves and left the dive. Suddenly when this group of small kids, say about ten or so, came out of the building right in front of us, it took me several seconds to realize that they were each carrying a gun and they were aimed at us."

"Christ." Hawk nodded, thinking of the looks on their faces; even for so young they looked older to him somehow.

"What happened?"

"Two of our men were killed right away. Lauren and I figured that they'd been as shocked as us and hadn't moved quickly enough. The kids kept firing on us as we scrambled to get out of the way. When I drew my gun, I knew as well as the men around me that we were going to have to kill these kids, children that had been sent to murder us. And my first shot rang true."

He stopped there. There wasn't any point in telling his brother that he'd killed two of them with one shot. That his bullet had ripped through the head of the first child and killed the one behind him. Hawk sat there, thinking of all the fucking shit that he'd been asked to do that no one, not even his mate, would ever know about. He looked at his brother when he said his name.

"Is this one of the reasons that you don't sleep well?" His question, put to him so quietly, tore at something deep inside of him that had him nodding, telling him that he rarely slept much more than an hour or two a night. "I can help you, if you'll let me."

"How? I've seen shrinks about this. Of course, they think I'm making most of it up, and after that, I quit going. I can't take sleeping pills, you know that. How is it you think you can keep me from taking a gun and blowing my brains out to get it all out of my mind?"

"Write it down. Buy you a notebook—hell, buy them in bulk—but write down the things that you had to do. How you felt about it. When it happened." Hawk said that would be a lot of shit. "Yes, it would be. Not shit though—it would be telling yourself the true meaning of you fighting a war that seems to never end. And even if its disjointed, who cares? It's yours to write. That you can name names should you know them. The way their deaths might have felt to you. How you felt when you killed those children."

"And then what? Give them to someone to publish? You know as well as I that's what nightmares are made of. Hell, I have them from the same shit. What good will it do anyone that I write this shit down?" He said he didn't care. "So you want me to write this for no reason."

"The writing down isn't for anyone but you, Hawkins. It's your tales, your thoughts on what you felt and saw. If no one reads it, it's fine. It's, as you said, for the best. You know what it says, what it meant to you. They shouldn't read it anyway unless you allow it. But you need to vent in a way that makes you feel better. Fuck anyone that doesn't care or know what you did for their country and mine. This is for you." He said that he didn't know if he could do that. "Yes, you can, Hawk. It'll not matter if you're angry when you write it or if you misspell words when you do it. I don't care if you write it all in crayon, just put it to paper, and I bet that you'll feel better."

"Should I read it when I'm done?" He asked him if he'd want to. "Not particularly. It's a lot of shit, like I said."

"Then don't. I think just the process of writing it all down, just how you want to, should be plenty enough for you to sleep better." He was warming to the idea. To blow up a notebook with all his dreams and thoughts sounded very good to him. "Then when you start to feel better, feel like you no longer have the need to write it down and you're sleeping again, destroy them."

"Yeah, I could do that. Easy." He already knew how he

was going to do it too. How he'd destroy each and every thought and bad dream that entered his head. Standing up, he hugged his brother tightly. "I should go in, say hi to everyone."

"They'll never know you were here if you don't want them to." He was tempted. Hawk didn't want to stand around and talk about shit with his family when he had a new purpose to work on. But in the end, he knew that if his mom were to find out that he'd not seen her, then she'd be hurt and so would he. "I'm glad that you're coming in. Reilly would like to see you too."

Hugging everyone, he looked around the house. Nothing had changed in all the years since he'd been here. The chess set, which he'd purchased for her a long time ago, cheap and made of plastic, sat on the little table that they'd used. He bet that if he opened up the little urn like jar that was near the set, he would find some chocolates that she'd give him when they played.

When Reilly hugged him too, he felt a connection to her that he'd not felt with anyone but Lauren. They were kindred spirits, Lauren and he, and he was sure that he and Reilly would be as well. And when she took him aside and asked him for a favor, he knew that he'd do it for her even if he had to go to hell and back to do it.

"I know that you get around and about more than anyone. Around town, I mean." He said that he walked a great deal. "That's what I was told by someone. Anyway, I'm looking for a really cheap car. Not anything fancy. Four wheels, a couple of doors, and an engine. I'm not picky."

"Boyd should talk to you about money." She asked him

why. "Well, when the two of you came together, even though you're not married yet, nor have you bonded or mated, everything that he has, it's now yours. All of them have done that with their mates."

"Why would he do that?" Hawk told her that was the way they did everything. They shared with each other. "I see. Well, I don't, but that's fine. I'll ask him about it. But I still need a car, and even after we paid for this beautiful home, it's going to need to have deposits made for the power and stuff. If you see anything, just let me know."

"All right. I can do that."

He'd talk to Boyd again and see if he had any plans for his mate. He couldn't think that Boyd wouldn't want her to have the best there was in cars or anything else. As soon as he was able to escape, he reached out to his brother and told him what he and Reilly had talked about.

Shit, I never thought of her not having a car. I'll take care of it in the morning. Thanks, Hawk. Did she say what she wanted? I mean, big or little. With the blood of Jon, Hawk had gotten the ability to read minds, and told Boyd what he'd seen there in her mind. *A bright blue SUV, huh? I can do that for her. You've saved me a lot of trouble. I owe you one. Thanks so much.*

If this writing things down helps me, I'll owe you for the rest of my life. Thanks so much for helping me, Boyd. He said it had been his pleasure.

As he made his way to his new home, he thought of his family. Hawk knew that he was luckier than most people when it came to family. Some never got along, and wouldn't go see them even if they were on their deathbed. Others didn't have any left, having either drifted apart over the years to the point where they had no idea where they were, or for that matter if they were still alive. Or they were simply alone. But he had a family that was there for him, even when he didn't want them to be. And the best part was, no matter where he was, what he was doing, he knew that he only had to reach out to any one of them and they'd take the time to talk to him. On any subject.

The house was lit up when he got home. He'd hired himself someone to cook and clean. And his cook knew never to make certain things. Hawk was never going to eat dried beef with gravy, never going to have instant anything on his plate, and ice was going to be in every glass that he drank from. He loved the taste of cold water.

Chapter 6

Joseph sat on the most comfortable chair that he'd ever sat in that wasn't his. He even moved around a bit, looking for and not finding the little pinch that would make him not like the chair so much. It was perfect, and fit his bottom like it had been made for him. And it was sturdy enough that he didn't feel as if he had to be careful of it so as not to break it. He thought it odd and sad that his only happiness for the last several days was a stupid chair. When the door behind him opened, he was almost sorry that he had to stand up.

"Mr. Dander. They said that you were here to talk to me. I can't imagine what we might have to say to each other, but I'm willing to listen. By the way, you fuck me over and they will never be able to find your body, understand?" He'd heard that Lauren McCullough was rough around the edges. Joseph had also heard that she wasn't one to suffer fools and told it like it was. He liked her immediately. "Have a seat. We don't stand on ceremony here."

"I'm here for two reasons. My wife, she wanted to be here too, but she's not well with all this. But that I will explain too. The first is about my son." She said that he might as well get his ass out of there if he wanted her to have Reilly not press charges. "No, no that's not why I've come to talk to you. I've talked it over with my wife, and we're not going to help him. Not get him an attorney nor pay any legal fees he incurs. He's on his own. We should have done that long ago, but...well, I just should have done it."

Joseph knew that she was shocked, but it didn't read on her face. Her foot tapped, just a little that he could hear, and she toyed with her fingers. It wasn't much, he'd bet that few would see it, but he'd been watching people all his life.

"He's going down for the murder of twelve people." He said he thought it was ten. "No. Two more have died from their injuries. A fifteen-year-old that was riding to his first ballgame with his dad. Also, an elderly man that had a broken leg and suffered a heart attack when he found out that his wife of fifty-two years didn't make it. Your son has a lot to answer for, and I hope to be a part of him getting his ass fried."

"As much as it pains me to say that, I had hoped that you would. But for the others, I'm so sorry about all of this. You have no idea how much my wife and I are sorry for all of this. She's ill now, my wife. The thought of something like him coming from her body has taken its toll on her. I came here to settle this, and perhaps ask that Reilly get help with all this." She nodded but moved her hands off the desk, hiding her tells. "As I said, we're not paying for his legal representation nor fees. But I wanted to give you something that Reilly's attorney will need. Ross is going to try and drag her into his mess, and this will help her."

He handed her the small thumb drive and sat back when she stuck it into her computer. He heard the sounds of Ross's voice and knew just what she was seeing — the day that young Reilly had been trying to leave work and what had happened to her that morning at her job when she had wanted to leave. He pulled out the second one and held it until he heard the last of Ross's voice screaming at one of the security guards that worked there to kill her, shoot her in the head so that she couldn't leave. His voice was manic, insane sounding, and Joseph cringed every time he heard it.

"This is very damning, sir. And not showing your son in the best light." He said that it didn't, no. He handed her the second one. "You don't have to do this. We have enough on him to put his ass away for a very long time."

"Yes, just for a time. But if I were his attorney, I'd say that he was temporarily insane, that the thought of not meeting a deadline for him had driven him to what he'd done. He'll more than likely get about five years and then be out again. This will make him not eligible for parole, and perhaps send him to a federal prison that he'll never leave other than in a body bag." She stared at him once again; this time her hands and feet were quiet. He glanced around the expansive office and knew that this was a place that got things done. Joseph looked at the young woman again. "Look at the recording and then you and I will talk."

When she stuck this one in the drive, he couldn't listen to it again. He'd heard it already, and it sickened him in ways that he couldn't describe. His son was a monster, just as the newspaper and the news on television were portraying him.

Instead of listening to the sounds again, he tuned them out. But he couldn't completely — it had been a looping nightmare since Ross had been arrested. Joseph thought of some of the horrific things about his son that he'd found out recently.

He'd killed a woman. Not just killed her, but had murdered her in a way that even the police had no idea who she was. Her body had been crushed to the point of not being recognizable as a body, much less as a person. And she had been one. A nice girl that he'd killed.

When he'd found his son's diaries of sorts, he'd spent three days reading them. There were days when he could only read a few pages of them. Others where he'd read a whole month of things that he'd done. But the details of the unknown woman's death had sealed it for Ross. Joseph would never help him in any way ever again.

The next morning, reading about Ross killing the young woman because she had refused to sleep with him had disgusted Joseph. Ross had taken her dead body and used the concrete roller that they used in the yard to run over her again and again, until she was nothing but a broken mess.

Ross had broken her arms and legs with it. Crushed her ribs and her skull. Joseph cried when he looked at what he'd said about it, how he'd had a release all over her body several times when he'd seen what he'd done. Joseph had wept not for his son, but for what he'd become right under his watch.

There were pictures too, of Ross and the bodies of his victims. His face smiling for the camera like they were on a trip together. All of them showed Ross covered in blood and seemingly happy with his handiwork. Joseph had thrown up several times when he'd seen that. And vowed to do all he could to get him on death row if possible.

"Mr. Dander is this recording from his car?" He nodded and told her that the recordings were sent to his computer at midnight every night. "I'm assuming that there are more. That he's done something like this before. I mean, having this recording of him.... He's literally happy when he thinks that Reilly is in the car that he pushed that day."

"Yes. I never bothered looking at them before this. I guess I didn't want to know what he was up to in his car. But I can get you those as well. They're not as bad, but you have only to ask. I wanted to tell you, too, that I spoke to Ross the day after he was arrested. There is a transcript of that as well that you can get. He told me that he was very disappointed that young Reilly had not been in the car. There were other things that he said too, but if you don't mind, I'd not like to repeat them to you." She nodded. "I called a good friend of mine. He's been there for me when I needed it, and I for him when he called. He told me to call you, to have you go over this, and that you'd know what to do. I don't want it out there that I helped with the destruction of my son, but I don't want him around either. I called Jarvis Wingate, the president. He told me that if anyone could make this stick it would be his best man for the job."

"He didn't tell me that you were coming." Joseph said that he'd asked him not to. "You were afraid that I'd turn you down if you set up a time to come here."

"Yes. And he said that if you did that, someone would come and see me to warn me off. More than that, he told me. You were a woman that got results. I needed to see you and to give you this." He leaned down to his briefcase and pulled out the first of many of the books that his son had had in his room. "Ross has been killing and maiming people for a long time. The first book there, Ross talks about how he had skinned a cat, keeping it alive until it finally succumbed to its torture. I have them all for you to take. I found them when.... My wife and I, we decided to rid our home of him, and we worked on the room that he's been staying in since he was born. They were on the shelf, right next to a DVD collection."

"Did you watch the DVDs?" He wasn't sure what she was asking and told her no, they'd only bagged them up and put them in the garage to take out to the trash when it was time. "I'd like them, if you don't mind. I would like to see if there is actual movies or music on them."

Her meaning made his belly churn. She thought that he'd recorded his deeds and left them in his room to watch over and over. When he stood up, she only pointed to her left and he made his way to a beautifully appointed bathroom. He didn't take in much of it because it was all he could do to make it to the commode to lose his lunch. Joseph threw up several times as he sat there on the floor. The pictures were bad enough for him to have viewed; seeing it in actual time would kill him, he thought.

When he was ready to talk to her again, Joseph rinsed out his mouth, then made his way back to the office. Joseph was shaky now; he'd been given a blow to his heart that he thought would never mend.

He was surprised by the man sitting with her. Jarvis hugged him, telling him that he'd been there the entire time but waited to see if Lauren was going to work with him. He told him that he was glad to see that he'd taken his advice.

It was too much for him and Joseph started to cry, sobbing out what he knew about Ross and how he and Evelyn were taking it. Lauren asked if his wife was at home and could she send someone there to get the DVDs, and he said that she was and that he'd call her. As soon as he got off the phone with his wife, he felt drained.

"I didn't want to raise a spoiled brat for a child. We were so careful not to give him too much or let him get away with too many things. We even sent him to public school, so he'd get an education in not just books but people too. I feel that we've exposed him to people he might have hurt without us knowing about it." Neither of them said anything, and he thought that was about the way it should be. He needed to vent, and they seemed to understand. "When I heard about what he'd done to Reilly, I thought about the two or three times that she'd come to see me about him. I hoped that she would quit working rather than to have to deal with him. Ross had become a problem in the last few years, and it had become too much for me even back then."

"That'll be brought up at his trial, I'm afraid." Joseph said it was expected. He would as well if it were him. "You should also know that Reilly is going to marry my brother-in-law soon. They've just bought them a house. I don't want it to come up later that we're all related, and you regret helping us."

"No, I'd never do that. I need this closed as much as you do. But as for Reilly, that's the other reason that I've come to see you. I didn't know that she was seeing your brother, but I'm happy for her." He took out the last of the paperwork and handed it to Lauren. "The house that she's paying on, it's

91

been taken care of. I'm not sure why anyone thought that she should have been responsible for any damage that had been incurred by the fire in the first place. The child had nothing to do with it, and to be charged with arson and to have to pay for the house wasn't right. But I have done some talking, and she has been given a full refund of the money that she's paid toward the house, as well as all her court fees. The real culprit has been arrested and is facing charges on what he'd done. Not just to her, but to the community at large. The only thing that they've asked is that she sign a waiver saying that she'll not talk about the settlement, and that she doesn't tell anyone of the second outcome."

"Why did you do this? You know who I am, what I do for the president. You know that I would have done this for her too." He didn't tell her that he felt guilty for all the things that he hadn't done for her about his son, but he thought that perhaps that she understood. "What happens to you, Mr. Dander? This thing with your son, it's not going to go away. Justice needs to be served."

"I agree, and I'm hoping that with you at the helm, you'll make sure that it is. As I told Jarvis when I spoke to him, this has been going on too long, and it's time that it ended. I really had no idea that it was…. It's much worse than…. I'm sorry." He pulled out his handkerchief and wiped at his eyes and nose. He'd been doing that a great deal lately, just bursting into tears. "You cannot believe what we've found in those books. And how he's just…worse than we ever dreamed."

When strong arms wrapped around him, Joseph leaned into them. It had been a long time since he'd had to lean on someone else, and he realized that he needed it more than he could ever have imagined. As he sat there, Jarvis holding him, he blubbered about some of the things that Ross had done. Telling him how very sorry he was.

"There is no need for you to be sorry, Joseph. You're making it right now, and that's what matters most." He said that he was trying to. "You've made a good start on this. Bringing all this to my girl, you've done something that no one else might have done. I cannot imagine how much this has broken you and Evelyn."

He looked around when Jarvis moved and sat down beside him in the other chair. Lauren was gone, and he figured that she was embarrassed for him. Jarvis seemed to understand where his mind had wandered to and shook his head after handing him a short glass of dark amber liquid.

"The DVDs arrived and she's going to have a look at some of them. Bear, a friend of hers, said that your wife was very helpful and that she's glad that you're all right. She worries for you too." Joseph nodded, his heart simply broken. "What are your plans now?"

"I don't know other than to bring this here. I know that the papers are going to tear us apart, and as soon as whatever my part in this is done, I'm going to take my wife on a long cruise, I think. And I don't think we'll ever return here." Jarvis thought that was a good idea. "Evelyn, she's as broken as I am about all this. I have to tell you, Jarvis, we had no idea of those other things. None."

"I believe you. And so does Lauren." He nodded and was glad that someone was on his side in all this. "I'm going to talk to my girl when she's finished here. I think we can make your part in all this just go away. Not the part where you've helped us, but the other, I think we can stash that someplace where no one knows. I know that Reilly will be grateful about your help on this as well. Not including the fire and what you've done for her there. She's a smart girl too, and she'll agree that you have suffered enough."

"I should have listened to her when she came to me those times. I was just then getting tired of my son and his trouble. But I never knew. I know that I keep saying that. Even with him living in my home, I didn't have any idea that he was such a monster." Jarvis nodded and said that he'd been doing it for so long, he got used to cleaning up. "Yes, that's what we thought too when we realized the extent of what he'd been doing. He'd gotten good at covering his tracks."

"You go on home now and get ready to go away for a while. And I mean a while as in, you don't return here. We'll take care of the rest for you." Joseph nodded and hugged the other man again. "You're going to be all right, Joseph. And give my love to your wife. But leave as soon as possible. Tonight, would be the best. But I don't want you not to call me. We've been friends for too long for me to just let you slip away from me. You have my number, use it."

After he made his way home, he and his wife began the process of closing down the house. There wasn't much to do; in recent years they'd had few staff and didn't go out much to social events. As they were boarding a plane, neither of them spoke of Ross or what they were leaving behind. This might be just what they needed. He knew that it was for him. Holding his wife's hand, he kissed the back of it and she laid her head on his shoulder. Yes, this was just what they both needed.

~~~

Boyd sat very still at the table and tried to wrap his mind around what Lauren was saying to him and Reilly. Ross hadn't just tried to murder Reilly, but he had committed a great many heinous crimes against countless people. Colin nudged him, and he glanced at his brother.

"Lauren is talking to you." He looked at her and saw that she was speaking quietly to Reilly. "Did you hear her when she asked if it was all right if we don't talk about Mr. Dander's part in the harassment charges?"

"That's not up to me, I don't think." He said that Lauren was talking to Reilly about it now. "Colin, what happened here? That man got away with sixteen murders that we know of, not including the ones in the terrible accident on the highway. How could anyone have missed this all these years?"

"I don't know. But as you were told, if you were listening, the things that his father turned over to Lauren are going to go a long way in making sure that he never sees the light of day again." Boyd nodded and looked at Reilly when she started crying. "Dander did something else for her too. Something about a fire."

She had told him last night what had happened. They had talked for hours about the incident where she had lived before and how she'd been charged with arson. Reilly started out by telling him why she thought that her name shouldn't be on the house deed. That someone might take it from them for what she'd been charged with at her other home. She might be right, he told her, but it mattered little to him. He wanted her name there beside his. Forever.

95

"I want you to own the house. It's only fair that you know that it's yours too." She shook her head at him and told him that she might lose it if he did that. "I don't understand how you could lose it, baby. It's a house."

He'd been going for a joke, but it failed miserably. When she turned and looked at him, he could see the fear and hurt in her eyes. Taking her into his arms, he held her as she started talking about the fire.

"I'd been gone all day when I came back to my condo. It was part of a co-op thing. I loved it. A nice house that was all mine without all the extra work of keeping it up. As I was getting ready for bed that night, I smelled smoke. Not a lot, but enough that I looked around my entire place and couldn't find anything out of the ordinary." She moved to the couch and he joined her then. "At three-seventeen in the morning, I was awoken with alarms going off in my bedroom. The fire alarms were making so much noise that I couldn't hear. And the entire place was filled with smoke. I was disoriented and confused as I tried to get out of what I thought was my house burning down with me in it. It took me a few minutes to get out, and when I did, the house next door was a total loss. People were screaming, and I was trying to see what was going on."

"Did anyone call the fire department?" She said that they must have, they were coming into the area as she stumbled out of her home. "Then what happened?"

"One of the firemen asked me if I was all right. I asked him if this was where all the smoke was coming from last night. It was an innocent question, but it put me in the middle of it. I was blamed for, at first, starting the fire, then later I

96

was charged with arson and something about me not alerting anyone that the fire was starting. I had no idea that such an off the cuff question would have gotten me into so much trouble. I was tried and found guilty of burning the house down next door." He asked her if anyone was hurt. "No. Luckily there wasn't anyone living in the house. But the owners had started their renovations on it. That too went up in smoke."

"How was that your fault?" She said that they told her that everything would have been saved had I called the fire department right away. "And if they had found nothing, what would they have done then? And why arson? That I don't understand."

"They found an accelerant that started the fire, and it was reported to have been mine. The fire marshal said that gasoline was used to start the fire and that it was at my condo. I didn't own a gas can. I had no use for one. But they found traces of gasoline at and around my place, and put it as the reason that the house burned so quickly."

He knew there had to be more to it than that, but she said that if there was, she had no idea.

Boyd listened then, when he heard Lauren mention the fire marshal. "You see, his son was going to lose the house due to being behind on the construction loan he was using to fix the house. And according to my resources, he didn't want that to happen—the marshal didn't want his son to move back into his own home. So, he found you confused and decided to blame it all on you. You were a scapegoat in all this." Boyd asked her how he'd missed that. But instead of Lauren answering him, Reilly did.

"They set fire to the house and blamed it on me. Even

going so far as to dump gasoline all around the condos when they were finished to take blame away from their son. The marshal knew how to make it a slow burn, and when I said that I smelled the smoke, he jumped right on that." She took his hand in hers. "How can people be so cruel to someone to make themselves look good?"

"I don't know, Reilly. I will tell you that it happens more often than not. But I do have something serious to tell you both. Mr. Dander, Ross's father, is the one that took care of this for you." Lauren handed Reilly a thick envelope and told her that was the refund money due to her from the house. "He and his wife have left the country. They're not going to be charged with anything that has gone on before because of their invaluable help on this case against Ross. As I told you, we have enough evidence to take him down, and all because of his father. You can't tell anyone about what transpired here, nor anything about going to him with harassment from his son. Without their help, we wouldn't have enough to get him to the point where he is never getting out."

He watched Reilly. This was entirely up to her how she felt about this news. He was fine with it. As Lauren said, without Joseph Dander there wouldn't be enough, and he'd gotten all the charges dropped against her in the home too. To him, they were free to do whatever they needed to distance themselves from Ross. But it wasn't his call.

"They helped me in ways that no one else had been able to. I'm sure that given enough time, someone in this family would have found it." She smiled at Lauren. "One thing I've learned about you guys is that you're on top of things even when you don't need to be. But I do thank you for this. Giving me the opportunity to do something nice for the couple that's only crime is they had Ross as a son. Yes, I'm all right with them getting as far away from this as possible. They deserve something to go their way, I think."

After everyone left, they sat in the kitchen and didn't talk. He got up to get her a glass of tea and she sipped it while she sat there. They had a long list of things to do today. Getting food in the house being a big one, but he was waiting on her. Reilly had been given a lot today with all this.

"I was wondering if you'd make love to me." He swallowed hard, trying to gauge her mood. "You've been really nice about waiting until I was ready, I know that. You even gave me the big bedroom when we stayed here last night. But I'd really like for you to make love to me. I've fallen in love with you. And your family, but mostly you."

He stood up when she did. Boyd wanted to kiss her. Just taste her. So when she came to him, her arms wrapping around his neck, her body pressed tightly to his, he held her to him as he took all that she offered.

"I love you as well. I think I have since the moment that I first saw you." She nodded and buried her nose in his neck. Every nerve ending in his body seemed to have been awakened with that and set on high alert. "You keep that up and we're never going to make it upstairs. I'll take you right here on our kitchen table."

The look she gave him, the way that her body seemed to come alive with scents, made his cat purr. When Reilly put her hand on his chest, just over his heart, he held it there for a moment before she tore his shirt off him.

"I'm not going to wait for you anymore, Boyd. My body is

yours—I'm yours. But if you don't make love to me, anywhere, I'm going to have to become the aggressor and take you."

He laughed. It felt like something just came loose inside of him, making him happy. Happier than he'd been in years. Then she bit down on his nipple, and he picked her up by her ass and put her on the bare counter.

Chapter 7

Her clothes were gone, and yet she felt warm. In fact, she was burning up, and she didn't think she'd survive him. Boyd was touching her everywhere, nipping at her skin like she was an all-day sucker, just for him. And when he opened her legs and stepped between them, she looked down at his own nudity and his thick cock. She reached down and wrapped her hand around him, hearing him moan out her name.

"I need you." She nodded and fisted him. The feeling of him touching her, just the slightest bit, had her scooting forward and taking just his thick dark head into her. "Christ, you're going to kill me. Let me fill you."

"Not yet. I need to feel you." He moved forward, filling her more. "You're cheating. Don't you want this to last?"

He surged forward, and it felt like he was filling her to her throat. His arms held her as he stood there, making her as much his as he was hers. He growled low, the sound of it humming over her body like a warm shower. Then Boyd moved, pulling back enough that she was afraid that he was going to leave her there. He pushed into her again, this time bringing her to a small yet devastating peak that had her begging him for more. For all of him.

"Please. I need to come. I need to feel the earth move under me." He grinned, his face looking like a man that had an idea, one that she was sure she wasn't going to like. "Boyd, I'm going to hurt —"

Her scream of release took her breath away. She saw stars and rainbows. Reilly came so quickly, so hard that she was sure that she wasn't going to be able to give him anything else. Then he leaned down and took her entire breast into his mouth and bit down.

There were no words that she could use to describe the incredible, delicious feelings that were racing over her mind and body. She could feel his emotions, his own needs that matched hers. Reilly pulled him up from her tender breast and nearly came again when she saw the small bit of blood on his lip. And when he licked it clean, taking the part of her that was warm with his love, she came again, a short hard punch to her system that had her limp with it.

"You're going to give me your all." She told him that she had. "No. Not even close. When I'm finished with you, you'll be putty in my hands and limp with exhaustion. And then I'll start anew. I will give you more than you've ever had."

He lifted her off the counter, his cock still deep inside of her. Boyd lifted her, lowering her again and again while he navigated the stairs. Twice he had to pause on the steps to sit her on the oak banister and take her hard, bring her again and again until she had to hang onto him or fall to the floor.

The bedroom door was flung back against the wall. She felt heated by the sound, like her body was responding to some kind of bell to make herself feel hotter, wetter, and closer to coming again. When he laid her down, joining her on the bed, it was like she had come home, home to a man that loved her without any doubts.

"You're all mine. Say it again for me." Reilly told him that she was forever his and held him close as he made love to her. "I love you with all that I am, Reilly. Be my wife, have children with me."

"Yes. All that and more." He touched her everywhere, his body slick with his need, with his sweat, sweet tasting to her when she licked his chest. "I love you."

Boyd's touch was like a brand to her flesh, his hands touching off emotions and feelings all over her body. His mouth was like a hot iron that marked her as his. And when he lifted her up a little, his hand cupping her ass, he moved faster inside of her, taking her to heights that she'd never reached before.

His mouth moved over her throat. And when he licked her there, as much as she had him, her body tightened in a way that she knew when she came she was going to pass out. The anticipation of having him come inside of her gave her need a spike, and her body responded accordingly.

When he bit her throat, everything stopped. Her breath lodged in her throat. Her heart, beating so quickly before, seemed to freeze inside of her chest for a few instants. Even her blood that she had been feeling rush over her seemed to have stopped moving. Just for a moment. Just a second or two, then everything came together.

A scream tore from her throat, seemingly coming from the bottom of her feet. Blood that had been stuck someplace in her body jettisoned to her heart and made it beat, what felt like a thousand beats per second. She was going to die, Reilly was sure of it. And when she came apart, her body just shattering when he filled her, Reilly felt the world center on him. Then there was nothing else.

When she woke, Boyd was laying over her. His heart, pounding as hard as hers, was right over hers. Lifting her hands up to wrap around him cost her more than she thought she had then; her energy and will to move were gone. When he laughed a little, rolling to his back, she went with him and Reilly marveled at the strength that he'd had after that.

"Christ, that was fucking fantastic. As soon as I can move, I'll show you how much I love you." She just stared at him, thinking he could not need more. "The next time we make love, you'll bite me. I'm sure that'll make it better for you."

"Are you joking right now? If that had been any better, you'd be scraping me off the ceiling right now. I have never come so many times in my life, nor have I ever, and I mean never, enjoyed sex as much as I did just then." She kissed his chest when she laid her head back down. "Now, be still so I can rest up. There is no way I'm going to be able to move until next week sometime."

He moved his fingers along her back, telling her what he had on his books for tomorrow. Boyd's voice was soothing and warm, just the tonic she needed to fall into a deep sleep. The blankets were pulled over her at some point, and she came to enough to tell Boyd that she loved him again. But she was exhausted and fell back to sleep quickly.

104

When she woke the room was flooded in light and she was alone in the big bed. A note on his pillow had her smiling hugely, and she opened it up to see where he had gone. Until that moment, she'd forgotten that he was a doctor and would be called in when needed.

Mrs. Davies decided to have her baby at two this morning. This is her fourth child, and I'm excited that she's finally going to have a son. I don't know when I'll be home, but if you need me, call the hospital, or you could reach out to me. Think of me and I'll be in your mind with you. I love you, Boyd.

It was just a few minutes after seven when she got out of the bed and made her way to the shower. They had purchased some new towels for this room, and needed to go and get more things, personal items, to fill out the house. As she stood under the spray, she thought about her dad and decided that he was going to be first on her list of things to do this morning. She'd have to get a ride from someone, she thought, and decided that she needed something to drive. Reilly was going to take Bea up on her offer to use her car while she was doing things today, and then she was going to figure out something for herself.

Going down to the kitchen, she found two boxes of cereal as well as another note from Boyd. There was a set of keys on the counter too. Picking up the note, she read it while she made herself some breakfast.

I ordered this for you yesterday, and they delivered it late last night. It's in the garage. Which, by the way, has an opener near the door inside this room. I love that. When I'm finished up today, I'll meet you in town and we can get some groceries. This might be fun. Love, Boyd.

She knew that it had to be a car, and was excited to have something that she could use on her own. Reilly didn't even care what it was so long as it was safe for her to use. The weather was getting worse every day. After eating a bowl of cereal, she pulled on her coat and boots and went to explore her car.

"Oh my goodness." It was a brand-new SUV, with four-wheel drive and four doors. When she got inside of the sucker, she wasn't surprised to find that it was loaded with every option known to new cars. The seats could even be heated, and she had a small television on the dash so she could back up safely. Excitement coursed through her blood as she tried reaching out for Boyd.

I could feel your excitement. Do you love it? She told him it was the best she'd ever had. *Good, I'm so glad. When I looked inside of it this morning before I left, I decided to get me one just like it. Different color. I don't think I'd look good in baby blue.*

Oh Boyd, I so love it. I was going to talk to you about it today. I couldn't keep borrowing your mom's car when I need to go out. I love-love this. He laughed, and it warmed her to her toes. *I'm going to see my dad and hang out with him. My shadow is going to be with me too. I wonder if Hawk had more important things to do with his time. But I feel safe. When I saw Dad yesterday, he was still groggy, but feeling good.*

I saw him earlier too. He's doing much better than I expected, and Mac said that she was going to move him to a regular room today, so ask before you go to intensive care to see him. She told him she would as she backed carefully out of the garage. *I was thinking that when I'm done here, we could meet at the mall and then do some shopping for food. There is literally nothing in the house. Mom brought the cereal and milk over last night, she told me.*

I did wonder about that. Oh, I'm so happy right now, I could bust. He laughed again and told her that he had to go. Babies were coming. *I love you so much, Boyd.*

The hospital wasn't far from the house—she thought they were closer than his condo had been—but it was still a hazardous drive with the snow coming down and traffic being nuts. She also forgot to put the car in four-wheel, and as soon as she did that, the driving became a good deal easier for her.

Getting to the hospital, she went to the desk and asked about her dad. Mac had moved him, but had also asked for her to call her before she went up. Asking about the phone there, she called the other woman and told her who she was.

"Thank you for calling me. I was wondering something after going over your dad's care. Will he be staying with you for a little while after he's released, or should I make arrangements to have him put into a nursing home? He's going to need a lot of care when he first is released. Bandages being changed, his blood being monitored, and things like that. It might be too much for you, at first." She told her that she hadn't thought of it but would ask Boyd. "You have a few weeks. I'm going to keep him until I can get his blood stable. Sometimes with a trauma like the one he suffered, it takes a toll on things like meds."

"I'm just going up to see him now. I thank you for putting

him in a private room, so I can." Mac said that she was family and they took care of each other. "Well, I thank you anyway. And I love this family."

"You'll learn that they can be a pain in the ass at times, but when the rough stuff comes around, there is no one better to have in your corner than them." She told her that she'd figured that out. "Oh, and I've talked to Boyd, but this Friday we're all having dinner at his parents' house to plan the Christmas day things. The holiday is in just a few days, you know."

"Yes, I'd forgotten about it, really." She'd not gotten a single gift for anyone, not even her dad so far. "I'll have to get with Boyd about that too. I'm afraid that I'm a little behind."

"Don't worry about it, Reilly. It's a big family, and they just enjoy being together where there is food." Laughing even after she hung up, Reilly made her way to her dad's room.

It would be nice to have him home with her, but that was going to be something that her and Boyd would have to talk about. They were new to their relationship, and while she was secure in her love for him, her dad was going to need her too.

~~~

Ross was sick of no one answering his questions. He supposed in their own way they were, but they weren't giving him what he wanted to hear. As soon as he was out of here, by hook or crook his grandma used to say, he was going to go on a murdering spree that would make the world sit up and take notice of him. He just had to figure out how to get out of this fucking cell and out into the real world.

The door opened and closed at the end of the hall. There wasn't anyone else in the cells with him—the two men who had been in the cells closest to the doors had left a couple of days ago. He knew by the smell that it was his lunch coming, and he was actually looking forward to it.

Whoever was making the meals for the prisoners today was really a great cook. This morning for breakfast he'd had creamy oats with brown sugar on them. Four slices of toast, as well as a scrambled eggs, bacon, sausage, and a glass of orange juice, as well as a fantastic cup of coffee.

The smells coming from the tray that was being carried made his mouth water and his belly growl. But he didn't move from his position at the wall. He'd learned that the hard way his first day in here.

When one of the guards came to his cell, he was to move back from the door as far as he could go. Ross had refused to do that the first couple of times and they'd told him to move back. Then on the morning of the third day, he'd not gotten up from his cot and was still there when the man came with his breakfast. He'd been tased after being told six times to move to the wall, and that had made him piss himself. The second time they had to take action against him, he'd had the same thing happen to him and he'd not gotten his lunch or dinner that day. He was careful now to keep to the rules.

Ross had a mental list of things he was going to do when he was out of here. But he had to talk to his dad about things first. His mom was forever pissed off at him, so he knew that whatever he asked of her, he'd not get it. When his tray was slid under the cell doors, he asked again about his dad coming to see him.

"I've done a little searching for you, not that you deserve it, but your family has left town. Forever." He told him that wasn't right. "Right or not, they're gone, and the house has been closed up and put on the market."

"The market? That house is mine." The guy started to walk away, and Ross used that to go to the bars and yell at him. "What happens to my things? I have all my clothes and stuff still in that house. Fuck this shit, I want my things."

No answer. Not that he had expected to get one, but he sat down and looked at his tray of forgotten food. His things were in that house. His things. And they were going to just trash it all. That was so unfair. And to not even tell him that they were leaving? It had to be a joke. A mean and cruel one, but a joke nonetheless.

Picking up his tray, he opened the metal shells that covered it up and looked at the burger and fries. There was apple pie, as well as a plate with lettuce, tomato, onions, and pickles on it. Small packets of mustard and other condiments were there as well. He was halfway through eating the best burger he'd ever tasted when he remembered what else he'd stashed in his room. His movies.

Ross knew that his father was too stupid to figure it out, so he wasn't worried that he'd find them. The DVD player in the living room, which was seldom used, didn't even have the correct time on it. No, he just didn't want them to fall into anyone's hands. Someone that would watch them and turn him in. Or worse yet, they'd try to do what he'd been perfecting since he'd been nine years old and killed a woman with the butcher knife in the yard. And then taken the lawn mower over her body until she was nothing more than a flat pancake of blood and gore.

The feelings that he had gotten had sustained his need for

a little while. But the need to kill was stronger than ever after a couple of weeks. Sneaking out of the house had never been a problem for him, and it hadn't been since. He could be and do whatever he wanted once he was beyond the people of the house.

Ross hadn't been able to record what he'd done until later in life, and he wished every day that he'd had something to make a copy of his first kill. The look on her face, the way that she'd tried to fight him when he'd slit her throat, was a memory that had given him the best dreams over and over.

He knew that he'd messed up by trying to kill Reilly. Not that he hadn't planned on killing her all along, but out where he was seen, that's where he'd made his mistake. But his temper had already been tested by his father, and there wasn't much he could have done there to make himself see reason. So, when she'd told him that she was going to leave, all his mind could center on was killing her. And he'd nearly done that too.

She'd been so fucking nice and sweet. He hated that about her most of all. And she was pretty. Her long dark hair, the way she would bend over something that she was working on, he wanted to walk up behind her naked and cut her head from her body. Several others of his fantasies about her had him jerking her hair so that her head would come up and he'd cut her throat that way. Either way, he had wanted her dead.

Eating the rest of his sandwich, he tried to think how he could get out of here and finish the job. There was no doubt in his mind that she was going to have to die. It was just a matter of when he got to do it that had him thinking about leaving here. His shit for brains father wasn't going to be helping now, so he had to think of another plan.

He backed up when he heard the door opening at the other end of the hall. Time for someone to pick up his tray. As he leaned against the wall, he wondered how fast he'd have to be to get to the man while he was bent over before he saw him move. Counting the seconds as they ticked off, he realized that he had as many as twelve seconds. He could do this.

But he had to be careful that he did it on the first try. He'd never get a second chance. Twelve seconds to kill someone. He knew that his upper body strength was very good. He'd been working out so that he could eventually snap a neck. Ross knew that it would take super human strength to do it, and that was his goal. Stretching his muscles, preparing himself for the deed, he moved around his cell and counted down the minutes until his dinner tray came. He had about five hours to get ready.

No snapping the neck. He'd not been able to perfect it yet, so that wasn't going to be the mode of ending this shit. Unless it was all he could do at the time. He knew that he could bang the guy's head against the bars, but how much noise would that make, and would it draw others to him? Things to consider.

He did pushups while he waited, but he was also judging the distance between the bars where his meals came in. Could he grab something off the man there, drag him in, and then kill him? It would be safer for him to do that. No one would see him; the body would be out of the way. And this just occurred to him—he could put the uniform on and be able to slip out of here without anyone being the wiser.

This was getting better and better all the time. If he kept to his plan, made sure that there was no noise to bring anyone to them, then he'd be home by dinner. Maybe his parents had left him alone to deal with this on his own, but Ross knew several different ways to get into the house and back out again. He'd perfected that as well.

When he heard the door open at the end of the hall, he knew that it couldn't be time yet. He didn't know if they were bringing in someone else to be locked up, or maybe his dad was coming to see him. No, that couldn't be it. They'd take him to Dad, not bring his dad to him. It had to be another inmate. But when the beautiful woman appeared in front of him, he felt his cock shrivel up and his balls curl up closer to his body.

"Hello, numb nuts. How's it hanging? My name is Special Agent for the President Lauren McCullough." Ross covered his cock up—something about this bitch had him thinking that she would kill him without thinking twice about it. "Move back, cock sucker, before I have to show you my way of dealing with fuckers like you."

He didn't hesitate but moved back against the wall. She sat down in the chair that he just noticed in her hands. When she was seated, he could see the shit kicker boots she had on, and knew that they weren't on her to make her look cool. She wore them to do some actual shit kicking. He also saw that she was armed.

"You coming here to do some hunting? If so, I'm afraid you're shit out of luck. Nothing here but me." Lauren laughed, and it wasn't a friendly kind that made him think he was humorous. No, this was a laugh that made him think that she knew he was full of shit in his bravo.

"Mommy and Daddy have left the country, so that leaves me to deal with your fuckery. And I'm going to tell you now, I'm not going to be nice or restrained with you. I'm going to watch you burn for what you've been up to." He just snorted at her. Ross knew that he was going to be long gone before he got into trouble over the car accidents. "We've been to your room. Nice little collection of DVDs you have there. It was really stupid of you to leave them out like that for me to find. Or did you want me to find them? Could be that. You're about as fucking stupid as anyone I've ever dealt with before."

"Those have nothing to do with why I'm in this shit hole. You can't use those against me because you had no right to go into my things and take them." She just nodded and watched him. Calming himself down, he smiled at her. "Who gave them to you anyway? I'm sure that you know you have to have a warrant to go into my home. Did you have one?"

"Nope." This was good, but she spoke again. "Mommy turned them all over to me when I asked her nicely. See, people don't believe I can be nice, but I can. Why, just a few days ago, I didn't kill this little cocksucker for cutting me off in traffic. My husband said that was showing that I'm becoming a good citizen again. And your daddy? He told us all about your little books. Gave them to me too. You are just too ignorant for words, aren't you?"

Forgetting the rules, he went to the bars and shook them. All she did was pull out her gun and lay it on her lap. Again, he didn't think it was for show, and that she not only knew how to use it, but she had. A great deal. He moved back but didn't say anything. Instead, his mind was changing his plans about going home. No point in it now; they'd taken his personal things.

"I don't know what you're talking about. What books and what DVDs?" She laughed again, and he wanted to lash out at her with a knife, cut her lips off her face, and then shove them up her ass. This fucking bitch had just gotten herself promoted to the top of his to kill list, and he was sure that she'd be fun enough to sustain him until he got out of town. "What the fuck do you want?"

Ross made his voice calm, his heartrate slow. Anger would get him nowhere. He had been good at showing no emotions. Hell, he'd never had all that many in the first place. It was just what it was, his way of thinking, and when something happened, he'd have to work hard at making just the right noises about shit so that no one would look at him twice.

"I'm here to inform you of your rights as a soon to be federal prisoner. You are wanted for the murder of sixteen women, and countless others that you didn't record when you were killing them." She stood up and aimed her gun at him. He'd bet there was never any hesitation from her — she'd kill and walk away whistling a happy tune. Nor did her finger leave the small circle that held the trigger. "As I said before, I'm going to enjoy watching you die."

After telling him all that was going to happen to him in the morning, she asked him if he understood what she'd just told him. Smiling at her, knowing something that she didn't, that he was leaving before this happened, he told her that he did when prompted again.

"Enjoy your last night of freedom, jackass. Tomorrow you're on my turf, and you'll soon learn that I'm not one to

115

fuck with."

He saluted her then and blew her a kiss. The woman was still laughing as she left him there. Ross was afraid. For the first time in his whole life, he was afraid of another person being better at killing than he was.

Now more than ever, he had to get out of here. Ross knew there would be no escaping the big house. And having his kind of fun was going to be next to impossible. All he had to do now was wait for his dinner and he'd be home free.

Chapter 8

Boyd looked at their cart...or carts, as it were. They were starting from scratch and needed even the basics of food items. His mom looked at her list and compared it to the one that Reilly had made. He was sure that they'd not missed an item in the store, nor had they forgotten anything. They had two carts, for Christ's sake.

"You're upset." He looked at Reilly when she said that to him, and asked her why she'd think that. "Because this is going to cost a fortune, and we've not even gone to get kitchen utensils or anything like that."

"Honey, this is all right, I promise you." He pulled her to him with his mouth near her ear. "We're billionaires. I own houses all over the world. The condo that I lived in before meeting you? We own them all and collect rent from them monthly. There are other lands that we own and rent as well. My brother Larson, he's the best at investing our money for us, and making us more money than we could spend in several lifetimes. So, I promise you love, we are just fine."

She looked at the grocery carts and then at the line they were in. Reaching over to the last-minute items that always got him, she pulled three candy bars off the rack and laid them on the cart too. He laughed so hard that he missed the first part of the words that Lauren was saying to him.

I'm sorry. I love my mate. When she didn't laugh, he knew something had happened. She asked him where he was. *The grocery store. We're getting food for the house.*

I'm sending people to you. Colin is with them. Don't fuck around with them, Boyd. They're there to protect you both. Ross just killed an officer and escaped. His good humor evaporated just like that, and he pulled Reilly closer to him. *I need for you to tell Bea and Reilly. They need to know now.*

All right. Should we go home? If we go there, we're going to have to have someone come to us to get supplies. We're without even the basics here. He saw his brother with seven men and felt his fear double. *Lauren, they're here.*

Good. No, get what you need now. I don't want you starving while we find this little fucker. I cannot believe that he got out right before he was mine. He didn't know what that meant, but leaned toward Reilly again and explained what was going on as Colin did the same for their mom. *I take it you told them.*

Yes. I should have thought of this before, but I'd like for each of you to take a taste of her. Reilly is going to be someone that he comes after. She told him that she was high on his list too, she'd bet. *What did — ? You know what? I know you. You pissed him off by being Lauren.*

Thanks. Rolling his eyes at her cheer over his statement, she got serious again. *Pay for your food and then they'll take you home. Right now the pack is at the house, along with some of my men. Bear is in the house, so don't be alarmed when you see him. Apparently, you have a lovely kitchen, and he's going to make dinner for you when you get back.*

I don't know if any of us will be hungry. She told him to act normal or they'd all freak out. *What the fuck is normal? Do you even know anymore? I don't. I'm supposing that he's armed too, right? Because why should everyone else be armed and not him? Does he have a car too? Maybe —*

Boyd, you're freaking the fuck out on me. Shut up and listen to me. He snapped his mind closed. Not on her, that would be dangerous to his health, but on the line of thinking he was going on about. *All right now. They're going to take you home and stay there. If you get a call out — is that a possibility?*

Yes…no. I don't know. I'm on call all weekend. I could call…. Wait, he doesn't know me. He has no idea that she'll be with me or any of us. He heard her cursing and he smiled. It wasn't often that anyone thought of something before she did. *He won't know to come to any of our houses, will he?*

Just mine, and I hope he comes here. All right, you're right, she's going to be safe so long as she's with you at the house. But I'm still sending them with you. I'm not taking any chances in this. You didn't see his work, I did. Christ, the man is the very thing that you would call a cold-blooded monster. He told them what was going on and why they might be safer than Lauren thought. *I have some figuring to do. Tell Colin what you just told me, and I'll talk to him in a few. I'm better at thinking on my feet than I am planning any day.*

Boyd didn't believe that any more than if she'd told him that she was a debutante and that she was going to wear a pink dress with bows. She was that good, the very best there was at this shit.

Loading the food up on the belt, he thought of how much fun they'd been having. How full the carts were, and the fact that they were going to have to carry this into the house and put it all away. He was glad now for the house with the attached garage. They could pull in and never get out until they were inside where it was safe.

Forty-five minutes later, they were putting the bags in the car. He and Colin were with the rest of the men, Reilly and Mom were in the cars out of sight. Colin asked him if he was all right.

"You know, surprisingly, I'm fucking not." Colin laughed, and he felt some of the stress roll off him. But he was still tense. "What the hell are we supposed to do to protect our family when maniacs and idiots come out of the fucking woodwork for our mates? And if that's not enough, we're all trying our best to have a fucking jolly Christmas, and this fucking fuckery is messing that up."

"Feel better?" He shook himself, trying to dispel some of his anger. "You do know that your cursing could use some work, don't you? I mean, what the hell is fucking fuckery? And a fucking jolly Christmas? Man, if Mom heard you just now, she'd take your head off."

"Yeah, well, I just met my mate, and now I have to make sure that some idiot doesn't try to run her down again because of her…. Fuck, her father. He'd know about him. That's why she left that day." Colin told him to hang on.

Shoving the bags in the car trunk, not even caring if any of the shit fell out on the trunk or not, Boyd wanted to get to the hospital and save his patient. But before he could run to the driver's side, Colin grabbed his arm.

"He's fine. She's moved him to a different room, and has enough men around him that it looks like a convention. And Hawk is with him too." Relief so profound came over him that he was dizzy with it. It was his father-in-law, or soon to be, and he didn't want to have to tell Reilly that her father fell down a stairwell but died in the hospital. "Lauren said to tell you good thinking, though. She was so worried about Reilly that she nearly forgot him in this mess."

"He's not going to get to her." Colin said that he wasn't. "I'm in love with her, Colin. I never thought, in all my life, that there would be someone out there for me that makes me feel like this. As if I could take on the world and beat it. But this, this thing with Ross. It scares the living shit out of me, I kid you not."

"Me too. He seems to not care about the consequences of his actions. And worse yet, he could have gone on for years and years doing this without them had it not been for Reilly leaving that day to go to her dad. She is the one we should be thanking for getting this monster off the streets." Boyd told his brother what Lauren had said. "I saw them too, some of them anyway. They're sickening. He's done things that.... He's done things to his victims, Boyd, that even as a doctor, I'm sure you've never seen."

And Boyd didn't want to either. He helped put the last few things in the second car and they made their way home. He was glad now that they'd gone by the dealership first to get his car. The roads were really bad today, and he didn't want to have to end up in the hospital too.

Pulling into the garage, he saw Bear there with a young puppy. "Found him wandering around. I don't know where he came from." As soon as Reilly was introduced to Bear, she knelt down to play with the puppy. "He doesn't seem to be afraid of me. I'm sure that he can smell what I am. I was going to take him to the pound when I left here."

"No, I want him." Boyd started to explain to her that he was a cat and they might not get along. "He isn't going ape shit right now, so he must not care that you're a big bad kitty that could carry him off in your mouth."

Picking up the little puppy, she told them to bring the food in please. Before he could think that he was the proud or not so proud owner of a dog, he heard her asking the dog if he knew his name. A dog was living with a jaguar. He laughed all the way into the house with several bags over his arms.

Bear started putting things away and he left him to it. Boyd thought it was funny that the big man was yes ma'aming Reilly like he did Lauren. And when he opened up the package of hamburger that they'd gotten, he was telling Reilly that he'd make the pup some dinner first. The little thing did look about starved.

The rest of the evening was spent trying to decide where things went. It was fun really, to have family there with them. Colin stayed for the dinner Bear had fixed for the men watching the house. In no time at all, the puppy—a name hadn't been established yet—was curled up on Reilly's lap in the living room and both of them were asleep. Colin and he went to the library to talk. He asked him how Ross had gotten out.

"When his evening meal was brought to him, he had a

plan. It couldn't have been spur of the moment, Lauren said. He planned this from the start. Pulling the guy into the cell with him, he broke his neck." Boyd thought about that. He was a human, and he broke a man's neck like it was nothing. "I don't know what kind of muscle it takes to do something like that, but the cop was dead before he could make a sound. Then he stripped him of his uniform and put it on. In less time than it took for the officer to even come up missing, Ross was out the door and into the public."

"Why isn't Lauren or the police around here?" Colin told him. "Okay, I can see that. Working for the president would cause her major problems if it got out that she was doing double duty. But damn it, if she was, you know this shit wouldn't have happened. There would have been ten guards taking his meals to him, and there would be a gun on him all the fucking time."

"Your anger is showing again." Boyd tried once more to shake it off, but he was just too stressed out. "How about the two of us go on a run? There are guards here with Reilly. Bear will stay in the room with her, and you have that big assed dog in there to protect her too."

"I have a dog, Colin. I'm a fucking cat, and I own a dog." Colin told him that he could have told her no. "No, I couldn't have, no more than you could have told Lauren. She would have shot you then kept the dog anyway. But giving in makes her happy, and that's what I live for now."

"Yeah, who would have thought we'd be the mushy type around a woman?" He went to the living room to check on his mate. Kissing Reilly, he told her where they were going. When she nodded and curled around the dog, he was jealous.

Of a dog.

Going to the door with his brother, they were shifting and taking to the snow in no time. Yes, he thought, this was what he needed. A good run in the snow with his brother.

~~~

Ross wasn't stupid, nor was he the type of person to get himself caught when he didn't have to. The thing with Reilly, that had been his dad's fault, and that of Reilly herself. Today and going forward, he was going to be calm and cool. And he was going to get things done.

His home was surrounded by cops. Not just cops, but there seemed to be an inordinate number of wolves hanging around too. Ross knew there were shifters around. He'd even managed to kill one once. But there were too many of them for him to be fucking with them, so he left them to the house. But he needed money and clothing. To get those, he needed to get himself somewhere he was safe.

The people that had been in the driveway had left about ten minutes ago. He had thought about killing them both and getting himself really calmed down, but there were too many witnesses around. The neighborhood seemed to be jumping with idiots going to work or some shit. He'd kill them when they got home, he decided. Inside their home.

The house had a puny lock on the door. In no time he was inside and going through the house. There had to be a brat someplace—the house was set up for it. Where it was, he didn't know. To his way of thinking, that was just one more thing that he could kill later.

Ross found the man's closet and then went to the bathroom. Time to clean the stench of the jail off him. After refreshing himself and dressing, he was glad to find some food that he could eat in the fridge. Sandwich fixings, as well as a few cartons of ice cream and some fruit. Almost as soon as the microwave dinged that he could eat, he glanced out the window and saw the cop before he got behind the tree. Well fuck.

Going to the small room that he'd found that coats and boots were in, he dressed for the weather and then went to the basement. There he found a nice sized window, as well as a sliding glass door that he could go out if things got bad. To him it would be good, he supposed — not so much to the cops. He was still trying to figure out what the fuck had happened that they'd been able to find him so quickly when he opened the slider and slipped out of the house.

The problem with trying to not be caught in this weather was the snow. His prints were leading them right from where he'd come out of the woods behind the house. Ross still had his gun from the cop, as well as an extra magazine. Killing one of the cops was going to be tricky without something to be quiet with, so if he had to kill them he would resort to the several kitchen knives that he'd managed to take.

He'd packed up a backpack that he'd found in the house as well. Money hadn't been plentiful, but there were other things that he'd found that were just as useful. There was enough ammo in the bedroom that he knew there had to be a gun or a gun safe someplace. But the cops coming when they did had messed him up in being able to find it. But the ammo would go a long way in getting him out of this town. After he took care of Lauren McCullough.

Ross had used the computer in the house as well. He'd

found that there were several McCulloughs around town. One of them was a doctor, another was some kind of farmer, according to what he'd been able to look up about each of them that were listed. When he got to the one that was the doctor, he knew that he was going to be the one that would be the most helpful in finding the woman that he wanted. Then it would be a piece of cake to locate Lauren.

Just as he was ready to pop his head out from the tree he'd been hiding behind, one of the cops came out of the same crop of trees. He was making his way to the house, and that led Ross to believe that they had no idea that he wasn't in there any longer. Laughing to himself, he made his way to the unsuspecting cop and cut his throat before he could make a sound.

The blood stained the pure white snow a nice shade of pink. But the more that he laid there, bleeding out, the redder the snow became. If he'd had more time, he would have played with the man, but he was being pursued and didn't have time to be caught. Not that they stood a chance—Ross had things to do, and they weren't going to get done by having himself a little fun right now.

The address for the doctor was only a few blocks away. After stripping the cop of all his guns and shit, Ross started walking toward the sidewalk that he'd been avoiding all morning. There were still people about, but they were no longer the residents that lived there. Now he'd bet that they were cops just like the one that he'd killed.

He didn't actually walk on the concrete that was clean of snow, but kept it in sight as he made his way around the little neighborhood. He was just coming up on the road that led into the place when he saw the woman again.

Lauren was obviously in charge. She was a dyke, he knew that. No man would want to be around a woman as butch as she was. Then he remembered that she'd told him she had a husband. Christ, he must have been a whipped pussy, he thought, and watched as she ordered the men around like they'd had their dicks removed.

Again, there were too many witnesses for him to take care of her. He thought about just shooting her from where he stood. Ross even took out his handgun and aimed it at her head. But he'd miss the fun he was going to have with her, and that was what he wanted more than Reilly being dead.

"Next time, bitch. Next time you won't be so lucky." He was still laughing at how easy it had been to get around her and her dickless men when he hit the main drag of the town. Ross had shit planned now, and there would be no stopping him.

Chapter 9

Boyd was still at the office when he heard from Lauren. She told him that she thought that Ross was on his way to him. He asked her how she'd come up with that.

He did a search at the house that he'd been in by using the computer there. We were lucky in that the family had a surveillance camera inside as well as out. The man of the house was headed home to confront the person who broke into their home when he recognized Ross. He called the police right away and they called me. Boyd asked what he was to do now, that he was at his office. *Don't leave there until I can come to get you. I think that I might have set this in motion when I spoke to him the other day. Just stay put.*

Gladly, but you should know that I have a gun. Lauren laughed. *Well, I didn't want to be caught with my dick out, as you were so fond of telling me. When you gave me lessons on how to shoot the sucker you also said to be prepared for the unpreparable. I think I get it now.*

Boyd, my dear brother, I think that I love you. If he gets to you, which I can't see how he would, kill him. Don't try and wound him because you hate to kill. It's kill him with a head shot or he's not going to have any trouble coming after you. And I do not want to be the one to tell Reilly that you got hurt on my watch. He said that his mom would be none too happy either. *Yeah, but lately I'm more afraid of Reilly than I am your mom. Not that I'm afraid of her, but you understand. There is a quiet deadliness about Reilly that is going to burst out soon.*

He hadn't noticed that, but then he'd never pissed her off, even going so far as to pick up dog food for the newest member of his household and a pretty blue collar with his name on it. Wendall was the reason that he'd been late going to the hospital today. The dog had to go out when Boyd was ready to go, and he didn't want him peeing on the carpet.

Boyd was looking out the window to the street beyond when he felt the gun to the back of his head. He wasn't stupid enough to think that he could not get shot here, but he was careful about what he did now. Putting up his hands, he turned around when he was told to and looked at the man standing before him. Hawkins had scared the fucking shit out of him. Boyd wanted to knock the shit out of him, and his quiet voice had him as tense as ever.

"That gun does you no good whatsoever if it's on the desk when you're over here." He asked him what was going on. "Ross is close to here. I've come to be a good brother and tell you to be ready for him."

"Why not go out there and blow his ass away? I mean, you're good at that, right?" He smiled at him, and Boyd felt the scariness of it all the way to the bottom of his feet. "What's going on here, Hawkins?"

"You're going to have to kill him, Boyd. Not me." He started to ask him why it had to be him. "Because I'm not here. I'm in DC working on a project over there. If I have to do this, I will, but it's going to cost me a lot of man hours if I show up on the news as a killer. The man I'm going after will see me, then I'll have to start from scratch in getting information for Jarvis."

"I thought you didn't work for him anymore." He said that this was special. That he and Lauren were finishing up this one project for him. "And you're going to kill a man for him."

Hawkins said nothing as he picked up his gun from the desk. When he slid the slide that took out the one in the chamber, he handed it to him, nozzle down. Then he faded into the woodwork. Not like he left the room—he simply became a part of the woodwork in his office. He was scary fucking magical, and Boyd had to tear his eyes away from the wall. He couldn't see anything that indicated that Hawkins was still there.

As far as he could tell they were alone in the building. He'd done what he'd come here for, thinking, as he knew he shouldn't have, that he was safe—Ross didn't know about him and that would keep him out of the line of sight. But he'd never thought of being searched for on the Internet, and that it would bring Ross to his doorstep. He was glad now that Reilly had stayed home to measure rooms for the insurance company.

The click of a door opening was loud in the office where he was. Boyd was sure that it had come from one of the rooms down the hall from him, and picked up his gun to hold it at the ready. Whoever was coming in, they were going to be full of holes as soon as they showed themselves. Boyd was a little on edge.

He saw the shadow before he saw the person. They were tall, whoever it was, and he could see the outline of something when he held it to his side. As soon as Jon touched his mind, he nearly screamed.

It's me. He let out a breath that nearly had him falling to the floor, he was so relieved. *I'm not coming in there until you're calm. But I've come to help you should you let me. I've already helped your Reilly. She willingly took some of my blood, and is excited and scared to be able to make a knife out of her foot. I asked why her foot, and she said that she wanted to kick Ross in the balls with it. She's almost as scary as Aunt Lauren.*

You have no idea. He felt his heartrate begin to slow down to almost normal speed as Jon came into the room with him. "You nearly had me shoot you full of holes."

"It would have healed." He stared at the young man who had come to mean a great deal to him. He would have healed, yes, but Boyd would have forever known in his heart and mind that he'd done the hurting of him. And for as much as he loved Jon, he would hate to have hurt him ten times more. "You're thinking too hard. I would like for you to taste a bit of my blood. That way you can become a chair if you want when he gets here and trip him up. If he's down on the floor, he won't be able to hurt anyone after you shoot him. You can be whatever you want or need."

"He's coming here." Jon said that he was very close. Within hearing him distance. "What is your plan for here? I mean, are you going to be something in this office as well?

132

I don't think I could take that at the moment. I'm a little on edge."

"You're a lot on edge, but you'll be just fine. And no, I'm not staying. I have some Christmas shopping to do. And the sooner the world is rid of this man, the better we can enjoy the day together." He'd completely forgotten about shopping with all this going on. He had something for his family, but nothing at all for Reilly. "She thinks the car is her gift."

"You're reading my mind." He said that he was too stressed for him not to be able to. "What does Reilly want more than anything else for Christmas?"

"She thinks there is no gift that anyone could give her now that she has you in her life. As well as a good home. And having her father on the mend. When Christmas morning comes, she will be content to be with your family and to be safe in your arms." Like a fool in love, he grinned. "You are a sap."

"Thanks. Wait until someday when you meet your mate. I'm going to have so much fun with you and her, you're going to hate me." Jon just smiled at him and put out his hand. "Will I really be all right here? Without your help?"

"Yes. And no." He didn't like the sound of those odds. "Take the blood I freely offer you, Uncle Boyd. If you have no use for anything that comes with it, then that is good too. But would you rather have it when you need it, or wish that you did when you don't?"

As much as he wanted to ask him what that meant, he heard the door in the back of the building open, then close. Taking Jon's hand in his, he used the other to cut a small slice across his palm. It seemed like a great deal of blood, but Boyd licked the wound and was glad to see it close. Then he just disappeared. Unlike Hawk did, he really was gone.

To appear as if there was nothing out of the ordinary, Boyd sat at his desk. There was nothing that he could be doing, but all he could focus on was that the man down the hall was coming for him. When Jon told him to shift, his cat consumed him like he'd been at a starting gate and the gun had gone off. He might have thought to be a chair, but he'd had no practice at it and was afraid that he'd only make it have three legs instead of.... Boyd stopped his mind from babbling before his mouth did.

As his cat he moved out of the room and into the hall. There was no one there, but he could smell blood. Ross had killed someone; he didn't know why he knew that, but he was on alert when he saw the movement in front of an open examining room.

Moving with the stealth only his cat would have been able to use, he nudged the room open and found it to be empty. Raising his nose to the air, he could smell that Ross had been in here recently and had moved out of the room after checking behind the door. There were three rooms down at this end of the short hall, and all of them had the doors open.

The second room was also empty, but there was no scent of blood in it. Moving to the next door he saw a shadow again and stilled his movement just as he cleared the doorway into the room. Boyd wasn't sure if he was just seeing things or there really was someone in the building with him. But as he started to think he was actually seeing things, he saw Ross.

He was covered in blood. His hair looked as if he had washed it in the blood of someone, then combed his hair so that it would look good with it. His back was to him, but Boyd could see the splatter on his pants from this angle, as well as how his shirt was torn in the back and there were scratches, long ones, that looked like a woman's nails had done it.

Sneaking up behind Ross, he could smell something else. Something that all his life he'd never smelled on another human before—the scents of the people who had touched him. Not only that, but he could also name the people, why they had brushed up against this man, and who the woman and man that he'd killed had been. Before he moved in to hit him with his cat, he told Lauren what he knew about the couple.

Where the fuck are you? He told her that he was in his office, and that right this moment, he was stalking Ross. *Why? What are you — ? So help me Christ, Boyd, if I have to come there and pick up your broken body off the floor, you're going to be praying for death when I'm done with you.*

I love you as well. He moved closer to the man, smelling his body odor, what he'd had for lunch, as well as the madness that was as much a part of him as his skin was. *He's killed two people that are right now in a dumpster on Twenty-First Street. They've both been killed with the gun that he took from the first man, a cop, and he has enough ammo now, at least in his mind, to take you down. And you are his target. Reilly is as well, but you are the one that he's doing all this for.*

I'm coming to you. Do not engage. Do you hear me, Boyd? Do not engage with this man. He's mine. Just as he was going to tell her that he had this, Ross turned. Boyd told Lauren that it was much too late for him to back down now. *Mother fuck and shoot the gardener.*

135

He closed out the conversation with her. Not because he wanted to, but he was concentrating on the man in front of him. Ross looked like he'd gone a couple of rounds with the people that he'd murdered, and that neither of them had gone down easy. Ross backed up from him and gave a little scream.

The first time he shot at him, Boyd was able to leap out of the way. The second shot, this one aimed for his head, only singed his fur. He could read where he was aiming, and when he fired at random, just firing at him like he didn't care if he hit him or not, Boyd stayed very still and only took one of the bullets. But not only did it not hurt, it healed as fast as the bullet popped out of his body. He'd have to think on that later.

He leaped at Ross with his claws extended and tore at his face. The gun was now empty, so his cat had no problems with toying with the man. Boyd begged for him to just end it, but it was as if he'd taken on a personality of a real jaguar and was playing with his food. The next time he leapt at him, Boyd told his cat to end it. As soon as he bit down on this throat, he knew that it was done.

~~~

Reilly was as calm as she could be with all this shit going on in her life. As she sat in the outer room and waited for Lauren to come and get her, or Boyd to come out to tell her that it was all right, she realized that she wasn't no way near being calm. Colin hadn't said much when he brought her here, only that Ross was dead, and that Boyd was fine.

Fine? She wasn't even sure what that meant anymore. But he wasn't dead, and he was going to come home with her. That's what she was told, and she was going to by God make

136

them let him. They had a life to live, and she wasn't going to see him behind bars. Not for her.

She thought about the visit that she'd had with her dad. Today he'd been not just awake, but he'd been well enough that he could talk to her. And the things that he'd told her had turned her body to ice. Ross had been the one that had shoved her father over the banister.

"I didn't know who he was until I saw the news report about what he'd done to you. And I don't think I'd ever met him before until I turned at the last moment and saw him. He mentioned something about this being his playground. I had no idea until that other woman came to see me. Lauren McCullough. She's really scary, isn't she? Remind me never to piss her off." Reilly had promised him that she'd remind him if he did her. "Anyway, when I told her what this Ross person had said to me, she asked me if I'd run into blood or anything in the house before the attack. I hadn't, but she said she was sending her team over there to check it out."

Reilly didn't even want to think about what she was checking for when she had a team looking around. While she'd heard some of the things that had been going on with Ross, she didn't want to know too much. Just knowing that he'd killed two more people before Boyd did him was enough to make her want to kill the man again. The officer that had first arrived here after she did came to stand in front of her. He looked embarrassed or pissed off; she didn't care. Standing up, she put her finger on his chest and was glad when he started backing away from her.

"You had better have something to tell me along the lines of I can see my husband now." He shook his head and she had had it. "You told me ten minutes. It's been four hours. You told me to be patient, that it would be soon. Again, four hours ago. Ten minutes ago you were here telling me that things were going slowly, and when SA Lauren McCullough came here, then I'd get to see my husband. That, as I said, was ten minutes ago. You either take me back there to see him, or so help me, I'm going to tear your nose off and stick it up your ass. That way you can smell yourself every time you fart."

"Reilly." She turned to look at Lauren, and was completely mortified that she was laughing. And she knew it was at her. "Reilly, would you come with me please? Boyd would like to talk to you. But don't touch him."

"Why the fuck not? You've had him all day. I need him, Lauren." She told her why she couldn't touch him. "What do you mean, his cat won't let him shift back? I thought that Boyd was the cat."

"Mostly they are one person. But when Boyd's cat killed Ross, Boyd sort of stepped out." She asked what that was supposed to mean. "Boyd is a physician, and his job it to save lives, not kill people. I think the cat is still protecting him from himself."

"You mean as long as the cat feels that Boyd might be in danger, he's not going to let him shift until all the danger is gone." Lauren said that's what she thought. "And what is the danger that his cat might be feeling?"

"I don't know." Reilly wondered if Lauren had ever said those words before, and decided that right now might not be the time to ask. "Even I can't make him shift, and I should have supreme power over him."

Lauren was the leap leader. When Reilly had first come

to this family, she'd thought it odd that there was a woman at the top of the leap, a bunch of cats, especially when she had only been turned into one and not born. Rich had told her that it was the highest honor anyone had ever had since he'd been born. After getting to know Lauren, she wondered why she wasn't running the country, she was that good.

"What can I do?" Again, she told her that she didn't know, but that they were out of options at this point. "And he has to shift now, why?"

"I need to talk to him. That's another thing. I can't get through the cat to talk to Boyd. Have you been able to reach him?" She said that she'd tried but was hitting a wall. "Yeah, same here. I don't know what you can do, but we have to get him to shift and talk. Otherwise, it looks like a simple case of Boyd waiting here for Ross so that he could kill him."

"Did he?" Lauren just smiled. "Oh, so he did. And what would have happened had he gotten hurt? I would have kicked you all over this building is what would have happened, in case you didn't know."

"You're stronger than anyone thinks, did you know that?" She told her that this was about Boyd, and he was everything to her. "Yes, for this time, but I think that you'd be that way if I was hurt too. Or any one for that matter. You're a force that I have to be worried about as well. After this is over, I'd like to talk to you about working with me. I have read your files, and you and I can work well together because of how good you are at your job."

"One thing at a time, please?"

Lauren led her into the room where Boyd was. The big jaguar was on the desk that had a computer on it, just lying there as if there weren't like fifty armed men around just waiting for him to make a bad move. He was acting like a normal little cat, ready to take a nap in the sunshine.

But it wasn't normal. The cat was covered in blood. His white chest was dark with it. She could see that it had something in its claws, and when she looked into the eyes of the cat, he pulled his paws under his body. She was told again not to touch him, but enough was enough.

Smacking him on the end of the nose had him snarling at her. When she did it twice more, he stood up with his hair standing and swiped at her. He was close enough to kill her, but all he did was swipe. So, Reilly hit him again.

"What the fuck is wrong with you, holding him hostage? Does it look like anyone around here is going to hurt him? No, they are not. His family is here, and so am I. You need to let me talk to him so that I can help him." The cat snarled again, showing off his large teeth as if in warning to her. "You don't scare me, you fucking shit head. I told you to let him go, and if you don't, I'm going to get a gun and blow you the fuck out of existence. I'm not shitting you. You might not be an immortal like him. Did you think of that?"

The cat laid down again, and she didn't even turn around but asked Lauren for her gun. As soon as it touched her hand, the cat disappeared, and Boyd was there. But he didn't look any better than the cat had. She went to him and grabbed him into her arms. Reilly heard Lauren ask them all to leave the room, that Reilly had this.

"I was so worried when they wouldn't let me see you. And you were being held here by that cat of yours." Boyd kissed her, telling her that he loved her. "I love you too. I'm so glad this is finally over. Are you all right?"

"You hit my cat." She said that he'd given her no choice in the matter. "He was afraid for me. He talked to me while he held me. Telling me that he and I were the only one that could have done this for our mate. And that I should be proud of the fact that I was the one to do it with him."

"Well, he scared the shit out of me." She held him tighter as Lauren entered the room again. "Here is your gun. It's a good thing that I didn't have to use it. I don't even know how to turn it on." Reilly handed her back her gun and Lauren laughed.

"You are definitely coming to work with me. And we'll make a hell of a team. And you don't turn a gun on, my dear friend, but use it like you mean it." Reilly asked her if she was serious. "Yes, about both things. You'll find that I never kid about weapons, and that having you come to work with me might just save me time in having to do the leg work for files I get."

"I don't know if I can work with you. You're not exactly someone that people want to be around much. But I'll consider it if you teach me how to turn that on and use it." Lauren slid the bar on the top back and a bullet came out of the top. Before she could ask her if that was normal, she pointed the gun at the wall and fired twice into it. "That's it?"

"Yes. And I'll pay for the damage, Boyd." He told her that she would too. "I will gladly teach you how to use a weapon. And so you know, you don't turn it on. It has no safety other than where your finger is, and when you use it, you make sure that you kill whatever it is you need to point it at. My motto is, kill or be killed. I think I might have that put on a

141

T-shirt."

They were still laughing at the joke when Colin came in with Jarvis. He was a man that demanded respect. And it had very little to do with him being what he was. People, she thought, just wanted to impress him. But Lauren seemed to not care who or what he was, she treated him like she did most everyone else.

"Jarvis, are you trying to get yourself killed by walking around my crime scene? I told you to wait until I gave you the news." He said that he had some as well. "What is it? And it had fucking better be important."

"I called Joseph and let him know that it was over." She thanked him for that. "Also, you should all be aware of the bodies that have been uncovered at the home of Joseph and Evelyn. Not just bodies, but animals as well. A great many of both."

"I'm sorry. I know that he's a good friend of yours. Is he coming back here? I hope not." Jarvis said that they weren't coming back. "Good. We'll put Ross in an unmarked and see if we can find out who the others were. How did you come upon this information before I did?"

"Hawk. And he has some information on a couple of them." Lauren thanked him again and Jarvis looked at Reilly. "I have something to tell you, my dear. As I have said, I've spoken to Joseph today, and he is relieved that Ross is gone. He told me that if I saw you again, I was to tell you just how sorry they are that this all happened, and that for them, they'd like to do something for you. As of this morning, you're going to be the sole heir of their estate. Before you tell me that it's not necessary, they would like for you to make sure that there is a fund set up for victims of senseless crimes, as well as helping out families like the ones that were hurt by their son."

"All right. I can do that." Jarvis thanked her and told her that he would relay the message to them. "But I need something in return from them. I need for them to enjoy their lives. To not think about me or the countless other people that he hurt in some way. He's been caught and taken care of. That should be the end of it for them."

"I will do that. And thank you." She said that she'd done nothing but said what was in her heart. "And that is just what they needed to know."

Chapter 10

Boyd was in the kitchen when his cell phone rang. It was a strange number, so he nearly didn't answer it. Saying his name, thinking it was going to be some salesman, he waited for the person on the other end to speak.

"Boyd?" He wasn't sure who the voice was for sure but said that it was him. "I'm naked and so wet. Can you come back to bed with me?"

He nearly killed himself twice running out of the kitchen and to the stairs. Not only did he drop his cup of tea all over the floor and slip in it, but as he was going out of the big room, he shoved open the door and it came back too quickly, face planting him right between the eyes.

Negotiating the stairs was tricky, as he had a slight headache and his eyes were blurry from the hit. As it was, he ended up not only in the wrong bedroom, but also the bathroom. He had to stand very still when he made it to her.

"Are you all right?" He nodded then shook his head,

145

and she laughed at him. "Oh, Boyd, your head is bleeding, and you have a knot on your forehead. What did you do to yourself?"

"I was coming to you." Boyd virtually crawled to the bed to be with her. After telling her what he'd done to get to her, he laid his head on his pillow and closed his eyes. "I thought it would be so romantic. You know, rush up the stairs, stripping off my clothing as I went. But all I did was get hurt and make a fool of myself in the bargain. Can you hold me?"

He knew that his voice sounded whiney, but his head was hurting, and he really did feel foolish. But once she curled her body around his, holding him tightly to her bare breast, Boyd felt better. She was his, and there wasn't anything in this whole wide world that he'd not do for her.

"I'm sorry that I got you hurt." He told her it was worth it to have her like this. "Well, I'm no less needy. But I'm willing to wait for you to recuperate for a minute. But don't ask me to wait much longer than that."

He was still grinning at her when he saw her breast very close to his mouth. Leaning over her just a little more, he was able to take the ripe little cherry into his mouth and suckle until she moaned. This was a much nicer way to recover than just being held, he thought.

She moved under him, her hips rising upward until he wanted to taste her. Why not? He moved down her luscious body, all the while nipping here and tasting her in other places. Boyd was going to take his time this morning. He had suffered dearly for this chance.

Reilly's navel held a special attraction to him. Swirling his tongue in the small indentation, he loved the way her breath caught and her hips rolled again. Every part of her called to him, but he was aiming for one in particular, and he was going to taste her there until she begged him to stop. Maybe he'd stop, he thought.

"You're hurting me." Smiling at her from his position between her thighs, Boyd told her that he was going to make her feel much better. "Boyd, I don't think that you can do that from there. I want to feel you inside of—"

Her scream of release when he bit down on her clit made him hungry for more of her. Her cream flooded his mouth as he suckled her there as well. Sliding his finger into her heat, he watched her face while he ate at her. Tasting her while he watched her enjoying what he was doing to her was the most erotic thing he'd ever seen.

Reilly rolled her hips, first trying to get away from his fingers and mouth, then coming back. Her words, in direct contrast to what she was doing, made him want more of her, to give her more. Boyd fucked her this way, his mouth and fingers enjoying every part of her. There couldn't have been a more beautiful sight to him than to see her like this.

"Please?" He raised his head from her heat. Looking at her body now, he could see why men wanted to paint women in the nude. There was never a better sight than a woman in the heat of passion. "I need you, Boyd."

"I'm giving you all that I can, love." She moaned again as he felt his cock ache with the need to take her, to fill her with his own release. "What is it you need from me, Reilly? Anything that you wish, it's yours."

He continued to taste her, to slide his fingers deeper and deeper into her sheath. Boyd wanted her limp when he took her just so that when she came with him, there would be no way that she would feel unsatisfied with him.

"Take me." He told her he was. "Then fill me. I need to feel you inside of me. Your cock a part of me like no other has been. Please, Boyd, give me your all. I want to bite you when we come."

He moved up her body, trying his best not to hurry, not to rush to do as she wished. And when he was at her breasts, he tasted each of them in turn as he slid his cock into her entrance. Her legs wrapped around him; not just around him, he thought, but becoming a part of him as much as he had her.

Reilly held him tightly, her nails digging deeply into his back until he felt her tear open his skin, his blood move down along his back. His cat seemed to be enjoying the way she didn't hold back, the way that she not just begged for more of them, but that she met them, stroke for stroke and need for need.

When she pulled his throat to her mouth, licking along his pounding pulse, he knew that she would bite him. That the two of them would be forever changed when she took his blood into her. And when she shouted out that she was coming, her body bowed up from the bed and her arms held him even tighter. This was beauty, he thought. And all his.

Her mouth scraped over his throat, then she bit down. He'd forgotten about his own release until that moment. When she suckled at the wound she'd made, Boyd felt his body poise as if on a great cavernous opening, then waiting for whatever was to happen, making his breath stop, his heart too. And then, when his own body came with hers, the explosions took him under.

When he woke, he knew that it was much later than he'd ever slept before. His body was stiff from not moving, his bladder full. Stumbling his way to the bathroom, he smiled when he saw the note from her. Picking it up, he turned on the water and pulled out a clean towel.

Your family of females called and said that they were kidnapping me for the day. Did you know that it's Christmas Eve? Me neither. Anyway, we're to meet you all in town later. Don't know when you woke, but I wish I was there to tell you how much I love you. Call one of the brothers to see what the plan is.

It was Christmas Eve. Christmas Eve, and he'd not gotten her a single thing. Hurrying now that he had a plan, he could not have stopped the smile from filling his face if he'd had a gun to his head. When he arrived downstairs to have a quick breakfast, he was completely surprised to find Bear there, making him eggs and bacon.

"I'm a cook. Before I started helping Hutch, I was a renowned chef, did you know that?" Boyd told him that he'd not. "I want to come and work for the two of you. I've had enough of the wild life, and I need to settle down and make a life worth living for myself."

"Why us? I mean, why not Lauren?" Boyd bit into the egg that had been put before him. Looking up at Bear, he wasn't sure what to say to him. "I thought this was just some eggs and bacon. But Christ, man, this is like biting into a bit of heaven and then having every present you've ever wanted given to you."

"It's the fresh herbs." Whatever it was, he wanted this every day. "Anyway, why not Hutch? She's a good woman and the best man that I've ever worked for. I never went into a situation with her that she didn't have all her information in a neat list, but she told us that she'd never hold back from us. And she didn't. When we were going into a nasty situation, we knew.... I digress. I need to make a life for myself without Hutch being there to pick me up and knock the shit out of me when I need it. You'll come to know that I suffer from depression. Not as bad as some, but I do have my days."

"You can work here for as long as you wish. And if you need help or just want to talk, Bear, we'll be here for you. But I would like for you to hire a staff." He asked if it could be vets. "I don't care so long as you trust them."

"Hutch would have my ass if I didn't trust them to be in your home." Boyd had forgotten that Lauren's men had, and some still did, called her Hutch. "And I talked with Reilly. She can make a man feel like a million bucks with just one of her smiles, don't you think?"

"I do. She's the best thing that has ever happened to me." Bear asked him if he had anything that he wouldn't eat. Boyd gave him a very short list of things, mostly to tell him that he wasn't much of a sweet eater. He said this as he was scarfing down a Danish that made his belly hurt. He'd been too full before eating it, and now felt as if he was going to explode after. He might put on weight with Bear here.

Wendall came out of the pantry then, a stuffed animal or something in his mouth. When he dropped it in front of Bear, the man picked it up, gently telling the dog that he'd been a good boy and threw it back into the pantry. Boyd didn't even bother asking. As a jaguar, he knew that he was going to catch grief from his family for being a dog owner.

Afterwards, they worked out the arrangement on where Bear was going to live—he had a home in town that he'd just bought—then what he was going to be paid. Nope, Bear told him, he—like Hawk and Hutch—was a long timer and would be paid forever.

Boyd went to the mall. He thought this might be the biggest mistake of his life when he drove around the parking lot six times before finding a place to slide his car into.

He knew what he was getting. It was just a matter of getting in and out before Reilly got home. But as he started looking around the stores, he could see a great many sales on things that he thought she'd like too. So, he began to fill bags of things for his new wife to be.

Fourteen trips to the car later, he thought that he had exhausted what he could get there. The ring was in his pocket, and he could not wait to give it to her. Also, on New Year's Eve, he was going to marry her. At his parents' home, right around the Christmas tree, with his family and hers with them.

It wasn't too late when he got home, and he was happy to see that he'd also beaten Reilly home. She had mentioned coming home to change before dinner, and he was worried that she'd do that before he got everything in the house. He had been thrilled to death to pay the extra to have all the things he'd bought today wrapped by seasoned people. Even more happy that when he started putting things under the tree, he noticed that Bear had put the gifts he'd gotten for his family there as well. Boyd had even purchased a few things for Bear, as well as Wendall. He was a sap, Boyd knew that, but he loved life right now.

~~~

Reilly had never had many friends when she was living alone, and even less when she'd moved here to live with her dad. Not that she'd been all that far from him when she'd moved out, but she'd been working so hard to get things the way she wanted, and had forgotten herself in all her life. Now she had an entire extended family that made her feel loved and appreciated.

Bea came to stand beside her as she tried to decide if Boyd would like the shirt she was looking at. It was really nice, and she thought it might be fun for him to wear to the office. He was the type of doctor that wore polo shirts, not a shirt and tie.

"Boyd?" She nodded and asked the older woman what she thought. "I love it. So will he. Did you get those other things you were looking at?"

"Yes." She thanked her again for the help. "I've not known him that long, but it feels like it's been all my life. Do you understand?"

"I do. And you'll have lifetimes together to get to the point where you finish each other's sentences." Reilly thought about the gun that she'd purchased at the gun and ammo store that Lauren had stopped at. "He'll love having his own weapon instead of using one of Lauren's. She has a great many of them, and I even understand the need for her to have them. But Boyd will like having his own, I promise you. What else have you gotten him?"

"A watch, because Mac told me that his has a cracked glass.

152

I asked her if it was something sentimental, and she assured me that it wasn't, that he hadn't had the time to go get himself one." She looked around for something that would tell her she should slow down in her purchases. "I didn't know what to get Lauren and Colin. They're very difficult to buy for—I mean, on such a short time of knowing them."

The two men with them had been very accommodating in keeping all their purchases taken to the car. The problem was now she couldn't tell if she'd been overspending by looking at bags. That was a good indicator to her. If she had too many to carry, then she was done. With someone taking them away, she wasn't sure how well she'd done. She voiced her concerns to Bea.

"Are you having fun?" She said that she was. "Did Boyd put a limit on who to buy for or how much you should spend on any of them?"

"No, he'd never do that. He told me that we have a great deal of money." Billions. And that wasn't an exaggeration either. Boyd had sat her down and showed her deeds to property that they owned, the stock portfolio that Larson had been working on since Boyd had earned his first pay check. They were very wealthy. "But there is no reason to put him in the poor house for one holiday."

"No, there is that. But if you were asked, even though you keep looking for the purchases that you've made, I'm betting that you can tell me just how much you've spent today, as well as how much on each person." Her face heated up to be found out. "Just as I thought. You're generous, but you're also very thrifty. Boyd is like that too. And the watch that is broken? Mac is right, it's just a cheap one that he picked up when he needed it. And I'm betting that if you asked him about it, he'd say that he can still read the time on it, so why replace it?"

She laughed with her future mother-in-law. Bea was the kindest person she'd met, yet she was scary firm when she wanted something. All the women in this family seemed to not only have their shit together but wouldn't take it from anyone either. She thought of the store that they'd been in earlier, and Reese's encounter with a bully of a woman and her poor son.

"What are you doing?" The woman, Beth was her name they found out later, told her to mind her own business. And with that, she cuffed the young man in the head again. "He's my son to keep in line, and I'd appreciate it if you would keep your nose out of things that don't concern you."

"No, that's not going to happen. I'm making it my business, and if you hit him again, I'm going to knock the shit out of you and walk on your body when I'm done." The woman was so shocked that she didn't say anything but stared at her with an open mouth. "He's been trying to tell you for over an hour, that's just how long I've been here, that he's hungry. Now you stop in your pursuit to buy up every god awful ugly pair of fuzzy lounge pants and pay attention to your son."

"You have no right to talk to me that way." She hit the young boy again, all the while looking at Reese. "See that? I can knock him to the floor and stomp on his head too, and there is shit you can do about it."

Reilly had started to go after the woman to lend support to Reese when Lauren told her to wait. As they stood there,

Reilly trembling in anger, Reese put out her hand for the young man and asked him if he wanted to go get a burger with her. He only hesitated a moment before he not only took her hand into his, but hid behind her when his mother reached for him. It was then that he screamed.

Reese knelt down to the boy's level and asked him what had happened. He didn't just tell them that his mom had beaten him with a belt before coming here, but he showed her as well. Mac looked at the wounds too and pulled out her cell. Reilly thought it was to take pictures, but it was to call the police. They were there in less time than she'd ever seen police show up for someone. But she had a feeling that it was due mostly to Lauren having a good connection to them.

"I want him taken to the hospital and pictures taken." The officer didn't so much as hesitate when he told Mac that he'd do that for her. "I would also like for you to make sure that he doesn't go home tonight."

"I gotta go home so they can eat." Mac asked Brian, the little boy, what he meant. "I got me some sisters there. I was allowed to go out today on account a I did the dishes last night without breaking none. But my sisters, they'll need to be having food. Momma tied them to the chairs when we left, and I told them that I'd bring them something nice and warm to eat. That's why I wanted to have something to eat, so I could save it for them."

Lauren sent three men to the house with cameras. The mother was detained until it could be checked out. Whatever the officers had seen at the home when they got there, Reilly didn't know, but Lauren had Beth arrested on an arm long list of things. One of them being child endangerment.

155

Beth had tied the three little girls, one of them only about a year old, to chairs without sitters so she could go out and "snag" her something for Christmas. There hadn't been a single item in the cart, nor the house, she'd been told, for the children.

Afterward they had spent over an hour buying gifts for the four children; all of them were going to make sure that they were well cared for after this. They'd spend the next few days in the hospital, Mac told them, then they'd go into a home that would care for them. After that, they'd have to see. Lauren had asked her if she would do a search on the children's father when they got home and see if he was aware of what was happening to them. Reilly said she'd be happy to do it. Now they were shopping for the family again.

"Do you do this often? Come to the mall on Christmas Eve to shop?" Bea shook her head and said that she'd not had daughters before. "I don't understand. Why would having us make a difference?"

"You're my daughters—maybe not by blood, but I love you all as if you were. And when I got the idea to go shopping with all of you, everything that could go wrong did. Today was the first time that we could all get together and have some fun. But I have to tell you, we might have to make this a tradition. This is the most fun I've had in years." It was fun for all of them as well.

When the last package was taken to the car, Reilly wondered where they were going to ride. Surely there were enough bags and packages in the limo to not have any room for them. But Bea assured them that there was plenty of room and that all the gifts were wrapped.

156

"You got them wrapped? How on earth did you manage that one?" She laughed and said it was easy if you had the right people to call. "What did you do? And is that why you had us write on each gift who it was for?"

"Of course I did. And perhaps next year we won't buy as much last minute as you've had to do this year, but we'll still have fun and we'll have more time to wrap our gifts. Or not. The pack was very happy to do this for us. I think they enjoyed it more than we did buying them." She asked what they were getting from this. "An education. Each of the ten seniors that are graduating this coming school year will get money in the form of helping pay for college. It is a nice tradition that we've started this year too."

They were about done when she realized that her feet hurt, she'd had way more fun than she thought she would, and she was starving. Reilly was glad now that they'd had snack breaks during their raid on the stores. But she wanted some real food, and she wanted it now. Laughing as they made their way to the restaurant, she could not wait until in the morning to see what everyone had gotten from each other. Reilly was happy, too, that her dad was going to be there with them, but he'd have to be careful. Life was full for her at the moment, and she was happy to be sharing all this with her dad.

The restaurant was packed, but as soon as they entered as a group, they were taken right to a table where the men were already seated and enjoying some appetizers. Reilly sat down with Boyd as she grabbed one of his wings and popped it into her mouth. She regretted it the moment that it touched her tongue.

"I tried to tell you." Her mouth wasn't on fire, it was burning out of control. Boyd didn't let her have the glass of water that was right there in front of her but handed her a slice of bread from the basket. As soon as she bit down on the soft warm bread, the heat in her mouth cooled considerably. "I love hot and spicy wings. It's the only way I eat them, and as I said, I did try to tell you, but you were just too fast."

Tears were in her eyes; the wings were still so hot, even though they were cooling. As she talked around her second slice of bread, she told Boyd that she'd have to get him back. They were laughing so hard with the rest of the family, she kissed him. But on the cheek. Reilly was sure that even his lips would tear her up again.

When they were finished eating, having all ordered something different then sharing what they had, Reilly was falling asleep when they were about halfway home. But as soon as they pulled up in the driveway, she woke up to see her home ablaze with Christmas lights and decorations. Bear was just putting the last of the lights around the garage when she got out and hugged him. It was going to be wonderful having him around all the time.

Chapter 11

Christmas morning seemed to take forever in getting there. That wasn't quite true. He'd been awake for hours, before the sun rose up, but Reilly was still sleeping. He had to laugh at himself a little. This was worse than when he'd been a kid, waiting for his parents to wake so he could open his gifts with them there.

The family had decided to have a large breakfast together, and he and Reilly were going there first thing. But right now, he had his own gifts that he wanted her to have. And while he had thought to give them to her last night, he thought that today, in their bed, was the best place to ask her to be his wife.

Watching her sleep had been a pastime that he had never thought that he'd enjoy. The way her lips were slightly open, as if she was giving him the scent of her all through the night. The gown that she had put on after they'd made love was sparkling in the morning light. And he loved the way her hair spread out on the pillow made him think of silk sliding over his own body.

When she stretched out more and opened her eyes, Boyd leaned down to kiss her. She smiled when he lifted his head, and she wished him a very Merry Christmas. He told her how much he loved her.

"This is our first of many Christmas mornings, and I wanted this one to be very special for us." She smiled again and told him being with him was special. "And for me to be with you as well, my love."

"When we have children, we'll never get to sleep this late on this day, will we?" He smiled again. "What time do we have to be at your mom and dad's this morning?"

"We have time. I wanted to talk to you about something." She looked so serious that he didn't want to make her frown. Rubbing her forehead, he continued. "I love you, so very much. And even though you have been using my name for a little while now, I wanted to know if you'd like to make it official and become my wife."

"That wasn't very romantic, was it?" She was laughing hard as he felt his face heat up. "How about I do this? I've been wanting to ask you for a while now."

When she sat up in the bed, then onto her knees in front of him, he did the same. Facing each other, she reached under her pillow and brought out a box that was wrapped in pretty red and green paper. As she handed it to him, he reached under his own pillow and handed her his gift. They were laughing that they'd both picked out the same paper to wrap them in.

The watch was something that he had been looking at for some time now. It wasn't state of the art, but more of an old fashioned one. The hands were there on the analog face, and he loved that all the numbers were there instead of the normal three, six, nine, and twelve. He was just putting it on his wrist when she said his name.

"There has to be more to this than you handing me a box." He said that there was and took it from her. "Boyd, I love you."

"And I love you with all my heart, my dear." Turning the box to her, he thought about the things that he'd wanted to say to her when asking her to be his wife. How he'd come to find this ring in the big barn that was his brother's. Larson had given it to him and said that it was perfect for Reilly. Pulling it out of the open box, he took her left hand into his. "The other afternoon, I went to see my brother about something for Christmas. I was just standing there, talking to him, when I saw something sparkle under the pallets that the boxes had been put on. When I bent to get it, I could see that it was a ring. But it was the design that had me shocked."

He pulled the necklace that had matched the ring from under the pillow as well. It looked as if they'd been made by the same fine hand, the same quality of work. Boyd put it around her neck, watching the way the diamonds sparkled in the room. But it was the single paw print that drew the attention from the gems. It looked as if it had been made from an actual cat, it was so perfect in its tininess. And it had too; his grandfather had had it put into the design just for Grandma.

"This would have been my grandmother's if she had lived. My grandda had a great eye for design, but his execution was off. So he had this made. Grandma would have loved you, all the women in this family, and been right there with you guys on every trip that you made." He looked down at her bare hand. "My grandda had the necklace made a few weeks before they both passed on. My grandmother had been in a horrific accident, and my grandda, not able to stand it without her, went to sleep one night and didn't wake."

"Oh, what a lovely story. Sad too, but so wonderful in their love for each other." Reilly put her hand on the paw print and smiled at him. "I'm assuming that this is his paw print on this. It's beautiful." He told her that it was.

The ring had yet to be taken from the box, so he did that now. When he slipped it onto her left-hand ring finger, it fit like he knew it would. The ring had been made over a hundred years ago, and it looked like it had been made just for her hand.

"Oh Boyd, it's so gorgeous." The band was wide, wider than he'd ever seen a ring before. And all around it were footprints of a cat. Even as old as it was, he knew that someone had taken their time in creating it, and he wondered why and how it had come to be. "You said that you found it in the barn? I wonder what other treasures your brother has found there."

"We'll go and see it when it's warmer. Mom and Dad had the cradle and rocker that were out there redone for Virginia. And some of the other items are being added to the house almost daily." She looked at the ring that was now on her finger. "I love you, Reilly. Will you please be my wife?"

"Yes, I will." She smiled at him, and he felt his heart take a tumble toward being more in love with her. When she looked at his watch, she squealed and jumped off the bed. "You've distracted me enough. We have to go now."

They rushed around the bedroom getting ready. When they came flying down the stairs, Bear was there with the keys to the car, and told them that he'd packed up the rest of the gifts last night. Having this man around was paying off better than he thought it would.

Going to his parents' house had been something that they'd been doing for years for Christmas. But this year, he knew, like his brothers, was going to be special. There were children in the house now. And soon to be adding more. His parents had been so overjoyed by everyone, they had said that they'd gone overboard on their gifts. So had he, he knew. Not just for Reilly, but his family as well. Last night had been so much fun seeing the look on Reilly's face with each gift that she opened.

Breakfast was just as it always was — loud with laughter and fun. Boyd had never taken much notice of it until now. It was just the way things were done, and how they'd been doing it for years before they had wives. But they were just as loud as the men were, and he had to laugh as his dad watched Lauren and Reilly arguing over something like he was watching a good game of tennis.

Lauren wanted Reilly to work for her. Reilly didn't want to be working with a pig-headed woman that settled things with a gun, as she described Lauren. And as usual, Lauren thought of it as a compliment. He thought that was a good description, but decided that it was the holidays and he'd not point that out. The argument went on for the rest of the morning. Then Colin stepped in to help.

"You are the best researcher that we know." Reilly asked him where he'd heard that. "Jarvis told me. And so did Joseph

Dander when he spoke to me a week ago about you. He told me that he was only a good lawyer because of the work that you'd put into each case that he had."

"I just look hard for things. It's no big deal." Colin said that it could mean the life or death of someone if they had the wrong information. Mac snorted. Reilly had heard about the trouble that Mac had been in with Lauren, and what she'd said to her about research. "If they have a computer and time, I'm sure that anyone could do it."

"But we don't even know where to start." Reilly looked at Boyd as Lauren continued pleading her case. "I have two cases right now that are cold cases for the police department. One is a man that died in his home with no gun or any other means of being shot. There was no residue on his hands to indicate that he'd done it to himself. There was no apparent break in, and his family all have air tight alibies. As I said, no guns in the house, nor do we have any reason to believe that he was in trouble with anyone. He was shot and killed, and there is no closure for it."

"And the other one? Is it a murder too?" She said it was a missing child. He'd been gone for nearly ten years, and his parents had never given up hope of finding him alive. "That's so unfair. You know how I feel about children. I love all kids."

"I know you do. But you never let it get in the way of what you're doing. You do the job, and once you're done, there are never any rocks left unturned nor any paperwork that you've not gone over." Boyd knew this about her too. When he'd been looking up something to do with one of his patients, she'd helped him find not just the information on the disease, but also how to compare it to other findings that he'd been able to unearth on his own. "It's a job you'd never have to leave your house for. I'd have your office set up with whatever you needed, and it would be updated and replaced as necessary. You could set your own hours, and there are bonuses, not from me but from the people I work with when a case is solved. Not the reason that I do this, but it does help a lot of people when the money is used for other things around the town."

"You're not a nice person. I'm sure that you've been told that plenty of times before. But I think that you should know that I am in agreement with them." Lauren smiled, just as he thought that she would. "All right. But on a temporary basis. If I can't work with you or you me, then we part ways as... well, whatever relationship we have now. Deal?"

"Yes. Deal. And you're going to enjoy working for me. I'm a pushover."

Everyone at the table burst out laughing. He did as well, thinking that this was either going to be a monumental mistake or the best partnership ever formed.

As they made their way into the large family room, Boyd thought of all the Christmases that he'd had in this very room. They were all memorable to him. And mostly due to the fact that every year since they'd all been babies, their parents had been taking pictures of them with all their gifts. Then the picture would be made into an ornament of some kind and the year added to it. This year was going to be too large to use, but Mom had said that she had plans for it. Boyd knew that whatever she did it would be epic, and just as memorable as the ones that hung on the tree every year.

He and his brothers had gone together this year and

gotten their parents a trip. They'd been saying that they were going to take one since he'd been out of high school. They had gotten them gift cards to use for restaurants and the cruise, as well as made sure that they were set up in fine hotels with fantastic restaurants at every port the ship docked at for the night. The look on their faces when they opened the box was worth every penny of it, he thought.

~~~

Reilly was glad to have her dad at the celebration, even if it was only for the day. He was being extremely careful about what he did and how much he did, and she was glad for it. She didn't want him to have any setbacks so that he'd not be able to get out of the hospital soon.

Sitting next to him after all the gifts were opened, Reilly knew that she'd been luckier than most. Her father could well have been killed that day had it not been for Boyd and Lauren looking for homes. She could have been easily killed too, by the same madman when he'd pushed her, thankfully, empty car into the traffic of the highway.

Her heart broke when she thought of all the families that had been hurt by Ross. And it would be harder on them this time of year to have a good holiday. Or, for that matter, have one in the future. So many lives lost due to one man.

When Dad put his hand into hers, bringing her out of her thoughts, she looked at him with a smile. He kissed the back of her hand and told her that he loved her.

"I love you too, Dad. I'm so glad that you were able to come here today. This is the best family that we could have hitched our posts to, don't you think?" He laughed with her. "Did you talk to Jon?"

"Yes. And I did take him up on his offer. But we're going to wait for a few more days before we trade blood. The trial is set for the new year, and Lauren thinks that it will go better if I'm not completely healed when it starts." She told him that she understood. "I never would have thought that they could try a dead man for crimes. I'm still not clear on why that's important, but Hawk pointed out that people needed someone to blame for this, and it was good that it was going to be done. I, for one, will be glad when it's over and things can get back to normal."

There was no normal, as far as she could see. Looking around the family that had taken them both in, she thought about what they were. Not human, any of them, thanks to Jon. And they were going to live forever too. Normal went out the door the first time she'd met Boyd and found out that he was her other half.

The children were put down for naps, at least the ones small enough to need them. If she was honest with herself, she thought she could do with a snooze too. But there wasn't time for that right now. Clean up had to be done, and the boys, as Bea was forever calling them, had a kitchen to clean up. Boyd even did the dishes at home, saying that he enjoyed doing it.

Leaning back on the chair that she was in, she watched the twinkle of the tree lights as they bounced around the room. The fireplace was a gas insert, but it was no less beautiful. Reilly was looking forward to making their home theirs. Putting things around the house that was a part of their lives to blend in well with the things that were there. Making it personal was what Boyd had called it. The house was perfect for them, they just needed to put their stamp on it now. Reilly didn't think she'd ever been this happy before.

There was something about sitting around a large fire in the fireplace with tattered paper and ribbons all round that made a person count their blessings. The family was sitting in small groups, talking about what they were planning or what they'd received. She had gotten so many gifts that she knew she'd be weeks putting them away. And Boyd had asked her to marry him. Nothing could be better than that, she thought with a yawn.

When she woke, the room was cleaned up and her dad was sleeping too. Looking around the room as she sat up, she smiled when she noticed that the room was empty but for the two of them. But she could hear them—the game or whatever they were watching seemed to be sparking some heated debates.

Just as she was about to stand up, Lauren came into the room with the president. "You're awake. I'm glad. I need to speak to you about something. I do hate to bother you today, but this is important." Jarvis said that he had something he needed her to do as he continued. "There is some trouble, I'm afraid, but I need to have all my ducks in a row before I make a decision on this. It's important too that you know that I'm glad that you're going to be working for me. It will make all of our jobs much easier."

He handed her a thick file as he sat down. Reilly noticed that Lauren had left them, closing the door behind her as she went. Opening the file up, she looked at Jarvis when she saw the first picture there on the top.

"Where was this taken?" He told her that was what he

wanted her to find out. "And these bodies, do you know who they are?"

"No. Other than what I've been told in the demands that were put to me. They say that they're one of the families that I've been using as informants, but there is something off about the picture. Lauren has looked it over, and while she had some insight on it, she can't tell me anything more about it than that they look like the couple and their child, but she can't be positive. And you know her well enough that she'd need to know one hundred percent that it was them before she acted."

She laid the four pictures out on the long table and looked at each one of them. There was something off about them, but what it was she couldn't see it right now. The next thing in the file was the demands.

It was handwritten, or so it appeared. But she could tell right away, by the font and the way that the words were put to the paper, that it was just that, made to look like it had been written by someone's hand. Putting it aside, she asked Jarvis some questions as she went.

"How did this come to you?" He told her that it had come via email. "And did you open this, or was it brought to your attention by someone on your staff?"

He didn't answer her right away and she looked at him. Reilly didn't know him well enough just yet to know if he was stalling or thinking. Then he asked her if she could please wait a moment, Lauren was going to set her up on the clone that she had of his computer at the office.

Lauren came in a few seconds later with two men and Hawk. When he stood at the closed door, she felt a finger of fear. Just as she was going to tell them she didn't want to do this, Lauren told her to look. The computer was running a video of the people lying on the same floor as in the pictures.

"I snapped the pictures off the video. As you can see, they're in their own home." Reilly was handed a picture of the family sitting in the living room that they had been supposedly killed in. They were laughing and holding each other, posed for the camera she supposed. Setting it aside, she watched the video twice before asking if that was all. "No, we have the letter that you have in your hand. It was a picture too, but he also had the original delivered to him via one of the staff this morning. These are only copies of these things. The real copies are being studied by the Feds."

Reilly started moving things around on the table as she went back and forth to the computer. She never spoke to the people in the room again. In fact, they could have been gone for as much attention as she was paying to them. When she asked Lauren what she saw, she told her, in detail, what she had seen in the video and the pictures.

"There aren't any pictures on the mantel. Also, I don't know if this is important, but the time of the year is off." Reilly said that she'd noticed that as well. "Yeah, the jammies are wrong for this time of year. Also, the mother has her wedding band on the wrong hand."

"No, the picture has been reversed. See the buttons on the man's jammies? They're on the wrong side. So is where the fire implements are placed." Lauren said that she'd not noticed that. "I'm sure that you would have. Also, did it say how they were murdered, if they were?"

"You don't think they were murdered?" Reilly told her

what she thought. "They're not dead? How did you come up with that?"

"Okay, here is what I've seen. Aside from the reversal of the picture and jammies, there aren't any decorations of any kind. No tree. There are no lights reflecting off the skin, and it's much too staged. When I was a child, I had special Christmas jammies that I only wore that night. These kids are not only in summer things, but they're not any kind of cute things kids seem to love."

"Okay, I see that now. According to the letter, they were killed last night. So that is wrong. What else? And Christ, you've not even opened the computer and you've found more than I have." She took her over to the computer then and showed her what she'd been running. "Where did you get that program? I need it."

"I wrote it for this kind of thing. The video is cut together from several others. In addition to the mantle being undecorated, the kids are younger in the video than they are in the picture. The mom has had her hair done too. I can get into her calendar too, if you don't care if I put another program on here." Lauren told her to do it. Reilly went to her purse and pulled out the thumb drive that never left her person. "While it's downloading, there is something else you should see. The video. The parents are breathing."

It wasn't much, the movement of their chests, but if you were watching carefully, you'd catch it once in a while. The kids weren't, but that didn't bother her overly much. Reilly pointed out that neither of the children were facing the camera.

"Why is that important? Not that I don't believe you, but why would that be something that you'd point out to me?"

171

She told her what she thought. "So, this entire thing is staged. Going so far as to put nose cannulas in for the kids to be able to breathe. Why? Are they in on this? Is the entire thing a ruse to get the president to make.... Christ, that's it, isn't it? They want him to make this announcement to discredit him."

"That's more than likely it, but without more details, I'm not sure enough to let anyone run with it. If you give me a couple of hours, I can have some of it for you." Lauren told her to take her time. "I'm going to need something else if I'm going to be doing this. I need a more secure network. I can build it, but I'll need untraceable equipment."

"You'll have it. I had no idea that you could write programs and build networks, Reilly. How did that get by me?" Reilly just looked at her. "Ah, so that's going to be something I have to find out on my own. I have to admit, I didn't have any idea you were so brilliant. I knew you were smart, but not this good."

"I'm better." Reilly felt her face heat up when Jarvis laughed. "I'm sorry. I'm not usually so snarky about myself."

"You are, but we'll just keep that between the two of us." Lauren asked her what else she needed. "You know you can have whatever you want. And it will be untraceable. I'll make sure of that myself."

After giving Jarvis the list, Reilly worked for another two hours. The equipment that she'd requested was brought to her, and so was the printer that she wanted. As she worked through what she was finding, she kept asking herself why. Why would these people, or the people that were making the pictures, go to so much trouble to discredit the president? But in the end, that wasn't hers to find out. She was the information getter in this, not the solver.

By the time dinner rolled around, she had everything that she could find out and handed it to Lauren, with the stipulation that she not tell anyone about it until she read it over. She had never done anything like this before, not really, and she didn't want to have any mistakes. Lauren was still laughing about that as she put the file in a safe. The two of them sat down and pretended that they'd not just worked on a murder of sorts.

"How did it go?" Reilly winked at Boyd and told him that she'd gotten the better of Lauren for once. "Don't let it go to your head. I'm sure that even as we speak, she's plotting to get back at you."

Reilly didn't doubt that one bit. It was going to be fun working with her. She wasn't under any delusions that she'd win a lot with the other woman, but it would be fun when she did. Passing the potatoes to Hawk, he winked at her. This family was going to keep her on her toes, she was sure of it.

Chapter 12

Boyd entered the small room with his file and noticed that the little boy he was seeing today was asleep. Lowering his voice to talk to the woman who held him, she looked up at him and smiled brightly.

"He's not been sleeping well. And I bring him here and he just falls asleep. I don't even know why." He touched his fingers to the little rosy cheek and was startled by what he felt when he did. Running his hand over his tiny head, he tuned the mom out while she went on about how exhausted she was with him not sleeping.

He reached out to Mac and asked her if she had time to come in and see the little boy. As soon as she entered, he took little Ryan from his mom and handed him to Mac. She looked at him as soon as she touched him.

"He's a little underweight, I'd say." Mac looked confused, but she didn't say anything other than to assess baby Ryan while she held him. "I can also see that he's not sleeping well.

Dark circles are not just for new moms, are they?"

It occurred to him that she wasn't feeling what he was and took Ryan back in his arms. Boyd looked at the mom, trying his best not to look concerned, and told her that they'd like to weigh him and do some blood work. He'd bring Ryan right back when they were finished.

Leaving the room, his mind started working on what to do for the small child. The touch had given him so much. More than he might have gotten if he had just examined the child. He'd have to talk to Jon when he saw him again, and find out just what he'd given him when they had exchanged blood that day.

Boyd was sure that before the blood exchange, he would have sent the baby home and been done with it. And in as little as a month the little man would have been dead. Letting out a breath so that he could center and calm himself, he looked at Mac.

"Jon, he gave me some of his blood. At the time I thought it was a lot, but I was doing something and didn't get around to asking him." Mac nodded but said nothing, apparently waiting on him to get to the point. "As soon as I touched my fingers to his face, I could feel the tumor pressing against the back of his eyes. It's not large, about the size of a pea right now, but it's hurting him in ways that he doesn't understand."

"Where is it? Can you tell me that?" He pointed to his eye and explained to her what he had felt then seen when he'd held him. "And you don't think it was there before? I mean, when he was in here last."

"I don't know. I didn't— What do we do? If we leave it, he dies. But how do I continue with a more thorough examination

176

when I'd have to tell her what happened?" Mac told him to let her handle it. But in the meantime, she was going to make arrangements to get him examined at the hospital. "All right. What do I tell the mom?"

"Boyd, you know what to tell her. Why are you freaking out?" Why was he freaking out? He looked at her and then down at the sleeping child. "He's in a great deal of pain, and exhaustion is more than likely why he's sleeping now. Tell her so we can get permission to operate if that is indeed what you saw."

"I did see it." She said that she trusted him, but they had to act now, not when he wasn't freaking out. "I'm not freaking out."

Mac just cocked a brow at him and he took little Ryan from her. All the women in his family were like that. They didn't have to say what was on their mind, just do one of those brow things and the men were ready to hop to do whatever they wanted. Boyd decided he wasn't going to allow any of his children to do that. It would annoy their own children when they had them. Or spouses. He was babbling in his mind, and snapped that kind of thought closed in order deal with the problem right now.

"Mrs. Shelby, I'd like to run some more tests on him at the hospital, such as extensive blood work and a few x-rays. If he's not sleeping well at his age, then there is cause for them." She asked if there was anything wrong with him. "At this point, I'd rather be cautious than not. He's a little fella and we need to find out the best way we can what's wrong with him. And since he's not able to tell us, we have to look until we're sure that we've done our jobs for him."

177

"All right. But can I call my husband first? He's at work now, but I really think if you're taking Ryan to the hospital, then he should know."

He told her that was fine, he was going to make a couple of calls then he'd come back to talk to her. It was the hardest thing he'd ever done, handing the little boy back to his mom without telling her what he knew. While she was calling her husband, he made his arrangements as well.

By the time they were at the hospital, he and Mac had everything lined up. They knew now what they were up against, and when little Ryan arrived, they started running the tests. Time would tell if he was wrong or not. And Boyd hoped that he was.

Jon was in his office when the reports came back. He'd been right. There was a small tumor just behind the little boy's eye that was putting pressure on his brain as well as his eye. He had to be in a great deal of pain, Boyd thought, and sat in his chair as he explained what he'd found, and how, to Jon.

"I didn't know what you'd get from me. I had an idea, but not entirely." Boyd believed him and asked him why he was there. "Well, I came to see the baby and if there was anything I could do to help. Besides giving him any of my blood. It's too strong, and I haven't any idea what it might do to his little system. Mine isn't cut, you see, but pure with whatever I am."

"I understand." But he had a feeling that he was missing something. "Mac is setting things up for him. All we need to do is talk to the parents, then Mac will operate. I'm going to assist."

"Yes, I understand." He stared at the young man when he stood up. "I wish that I could help you, Uncle Boyd, but you

178

know that I can't. As I said, my blood is too powerful by itself. Being that it's not diluted or anything."

"Jon, do you think this is going to be ongoing? Me only having to touch someone to tell what is wrong with them? It would be helpful for me and my patients, but also a little scary. What do you think?"

"I would imagine that it will always be there. When you touched Ryan, what did you feel? The first thing?" He told him that he felt a little freaked out. "No, before you found the tumor in his head, what did you feel when you touched him?"

He had to think about that for a minute. By the time he realized that he'd felt a calmness that he'd never felt around a patient before, his office door was closed and he was sitting there all by himself. Looking at the file on his desk, he wondered where it had come from. Then he remembered that the nurse had brought it to him before all this happened.

After the brief knock at the door, Mac came in to tell him what she'd been doing and was now ready to begin when he was. But he kept thinking about Jon's comments. She asked him what was bothering him.

"I don't know. Jon was here a few minutes ago, and he said some things that were sort of cryptic. I think he was trying to tell me something, but I can't figure it out." Boyd told Mac what he'd said and why he couldn't help the little boy. "What do you suppose he meant?"

"I don't know. But I should have warned you that his blood is really strong—I would have had you cut it before tasting it if I had been there with you." He looked at her when she said that. "What?"

"Cut it. We have to cut it to save him." She looked confused and he stood up, smiling. "He can't tell us everything. Something about rules and not changing the future about things. But he said that he couldn't help because his blood was much too strong."

"Okay. But I'm still clueless about what you're saying."

All he did to explain was hand her Ryan's file. He left her there, laughing at how long it had taken him to figure it out. He was going to hug that kid when he got home.

Just as he was going in the nursery from the office he'd been in, he heard her laughing. It had taken her longer than it had him, but he was all right with that. Like Reilly, he wasn't going to be expecting to be one up on his family, but when he was, he was going to enjoy the moment.

He asked to examine Ryan once more. The staff was more than willing to help him as he'd been a long-time doctor there, since he'd been out of med school. Picking the baby up, he held him to him for a little while and then looked down at him.

Boyd could see the pain in his eyes. Ryan had dark circles under his little eyes, and his cheeks weren't rosy like one would expect from a six-month-old. Mac joined him when he was ready to give him some of his blood, and she pulled out a scalpel that was still in the packaging.

"No point in taking chances at this point. How much are you going to give him?" Boyd told her that he'd only give him drops, then wait between each of them to see whether or not it was working. "Good idea. But I think we should take turns giving him some of each of our blood. I don't know what it would do if he were to get too much of one of us."

"I think you might be right."

She slid the sharp instrument across his thumb after cleaning it with a swab, and he watched his blood come to the surface. Putting it in the little boy's mouth, he wasn't surprised that he suckled it like a bottle. When he thought that he'd had enough, he pulled away and watched him.

The change was noticeable right away. The pained look was still there, but his cheeks were no longer dried and chapped looking. This time it was Mac who held Ryan, and Boyd did the cutting. As soon as he closed his eyes, Boyd put his hand on his head and "looked" for the tumor again.

There was nothing there. Not even any pain that he'd felt the first time he'd touched Ryan's head. As Mac held him, Boyd asked about giving him just a little more just to make sure that it wasn't so small that he'd not felt it.

"I have a better idea. I think you should take his blood. That way, you can sort of look around once in a while to make sure."

He told her that was an excellent idea and licked his little heel, and using another scalpel, he cut the tiniest little cut there and tasted his blood. He could now look at where the tumor had been and could see that it was completely gone.

After another hour of watching him, still running tests to make sure that nothing was missed, Boyd released Ryan to his parents, who were happy to see his color had returned to normal and his appetite had returned. All in all, Boyd thought it was a good day. He only hoped that there were more like this in the future.

~~~

Ronny wasn't sure what to do with himself. He'd been in

181

nice homes before—it was part of his job, he supposed. But this house was much nicer than he'd ever had the pleasure of being in. And it was a very understated wealth too. Not a shoved in your face, I have it all kind of place like he'd seen before.

He knew that Reilly was working on something for the family. He'd woken up to a strange room, and it took him a few seconds to realize where he was and what had happened. Since he'd been hurt, he was afraid now almost every time he closed his eyes. The feeling of falling would make him cry out when he woke. Ronny looked at the man who had been sitting with him since he woke.

"You need anything? I have to tell you, that daughter of yours, she's a pistol, ain't she?" He grinned and told Mr. McCullough that he was right about that. "No need to be formal around us. We're family, you know. And maybe soon we can share a grandbaby or two, or a dozen."

"She's been living with me for a few months now. Necessity, really, but it's been wonderful having her around. I never realized how lonely I was until she was there for me all the time. And she keeps me in line as well." Rich said that his wife did the same thing, and his daughters-in-law didn't cut him any slack either. "You'd think they'd have a little more respect for us, wouldn't you? I mean, we're older and a good deal smarter. Not really, but I don't think we'll share that with them."

They both laughed, and Rich handed him a glass of tea that had been sitting on the tray. There were other treats too, and when he was given a plate of cookies, he thought he'd died and gone to heaven because they were so good.

"Reese. She's about the best thing that has happened here with her cooking and all. And boy oh boy, can she bake. Most of what you had for breakfast, that was her. She got herself a restaurant now. My son and grandson got it for her for Christmas." A restaurant. Who gave entire restaurants to someone for Christmas and never thought a thing about it? "You going to be staying around here then, I heard. Good for you. They'll have you up and around in no time."

"I have a house and a job, but I'm going to be staying with my daughter until I'm up and around better. I'm not sure how long I'll be there." Rich nodded and told him that he had options, and that was a good thing. "I'm to understand that Reilly is going to be working for Lauren. She's scary, isn't she? I mean, a little."

"She's terrifying is what she is. Good as gold when it suits her, but she has herself a temper too." Ronny said that she frightened him every time she came into the room. "Yes, sir. You'll learn to be all right with her around. As you said, she can be scary, but she'll protect you like you're her own kid. And she's the leap leader too. Couldn't have been prouder of her than if it had been my own son to take the leap."

Ronny had heard that too. That she had whipped the leap into shape in a few days, and had made sure that they knew not to fuck with her, as his daughter told him. He wondered what sort of man could let his wife do that and feel good about it. Ronny thought that Colin was the perfect match for the intense woman. He was so laid back, he'd have to check his pulse when things were going on. Not really, but his mom used to say that about lazy people and he'd thought of it just then.

183

"She told me that she was working for Lauren and that she was on a case with her. That's the reason that she's been in and out a great deal." Ronny had been brought here earlier this morning so that Reilly could go into town. He'd told her that he'd be fine at home, but she had him bundled up and had him here before he could point out that he'd been living alone for a long time now. "I'm sorry to have imposed on you today."

"Imposed? My goodness, it's nice to have another man to talk to after all them women around. I tell you, I was sure that they were going to put ribbons and bows all over this house when they came to decorate. Then I got to thinking about that and realized that not a one of them is the ribbon and bow sort of person." Ronny laughed hard, and had to hold onto his wounds when they pulled a bit. "You coming over here is a good thing for me too. Got me out of having to go to the mall to do after Christmas shopping. I hate shopping anyway, and being at the mall for a sale, that ain't my way of spending the day."

The two of them talked about different things. Rich told him that he was going to go fishing as soon as there was a break in the snow. It wasn't even January yet, so he was thinking the man was going ice fishing or something. Then they got around to talking about being a cat.

"When I was born, it was a different time than it is now. Virginia, you met her, she's a famous author, and she wrote some pretty racy stories about our kind even before she realized that we were a real thing." He said that Reilly told him that she was going on a book signing in Europe early next year. "Yes, about the time we're going to be on our cruise. We might just pop on over there and see her then. She's not much for people either. Anyway, we were to keep to ourselves and not let anyone know what we were. It was scary then, not trusting anyone. My dad, he died after my mom did when she was in a car accident that took her life. That kind of love, that's not anything that humans understand. I don't think."

"Reilly's mom wasn't one to be kind to anyone. She was when we first got married. Then she got a taste for money. I've had some all my life, saving whenever I could, stashing away here and there. But once she found out about it, it was like she turned into a different person." He thought of all the arguments they'd had over money. "When she found out that she was carrying Reilly, May, my wife wanted me to spend every dime on her to keep her happy. It didn't work out. She wasn't ever going to be happy. And then I told her that the money would go to the baby, for its education. After Reilly was born, a couple of days later, she up and left me, and then divorced me a few years later when she found herself someone else that would spend money on her."

"I'm sorry to hear that, I am. But you don't seem any worse for wear about it, and you did a good job in raising Reilly by yourself. She's working on making a name for herself with this help that she's doing for Lauren. The rest of the girls, they have jobs on their own." Ronny thanked him for that. "No need for that. A man thinks that he's going to be lucky if one of his sons does well in finding himself someone. I got me five of the most incredible women a man could want. A surgeon, cook, author. I got me one that has the ear of the president. And your daughter, she fits right in there with them. A man couldn't do any better than I have."

185

"I'm to understand that Hawkins is the last of your sons that hasn't found his other half. Do you think that will happen soon?" Ronny wasn't sure that he was going to answer him. The man looked somewhat sad about it. "I'm sorry. I didn't mean to bring up something that is none of my business."

"You're family, Ronny. You can't be thinking that when you have a question. But Hawkins. I'm hoping that he finds his other half. But he is going to be a hard man to love, I'm thinking. He's seen too much and done more than that." Ronny had noticed that the man had a haunted look about him. And he was quiet too. "His mate, she's going to need herself some backbone to put up with him. He's a little moody, and can't stand to be around people all that much. Not even us. While I know that we can be a bit much on anyone, Hawkins will disappear for days on end when he's had enough of us."

"When he was talking to me at Christmas, he told me that he'd just gotten out of the service but that he still did some work for them." Rich nodded and said that he did. "He seems to get along best with Reilly. I don't know why I think that, but they seem to gravitate to each other a great deal."

"I noticed that too. They can sit for a spell and not say a word to each other, and it somehow makes them both feel better. When Reilly first came here, it was Hawkins that kept her from doing something rash. Having that fool out there trying to kill her, he kept her safe and sound." Ronny shivered when he thought of Ross Dander. "He's gone now, did you know that? Boyd, he took care of him in the only way that is possible for our kind."

"I heard." He had heard a great deal about it, and decided that he'd stay on their good side even if he had to run away to keep from pissing them off. Smiling, he asked Rich how they took care of the body.

"They thought that he'd gotten in a car accident which is all right with me. I would have liked to have had a piece of him myself. But, as I said, Boyd took care of his mate." As far as a son-in-law went, Ronny really liked the young man. And he made his Reilly happy. "You heard that the business with that house fire has been taken care of, haven't you? I've been thinking on that some. Why do you suppose Reilly didn't go searching for that all on her own?"

"She did." Ronny thought of the day she'd told him what had really happened that night. "Reilly said that if she showed up with the evidence on the fire, everyone would think that she had made it up. That she'd forged things to make herself look innocent. And she had a reputation to maintain. One that would pay the bills for her after this was all done and she could make herself into something. I don't think she counted on losing her job over it or having everything that she owned taken from her. When she came home, it was a blessing for me, but to her, she was a failure. So, when she got the research job working for Dander, she felt like she was going to be all right, even if she was broke most of the time."

"Self-worth." Ronny nodded at Rich. "She's been working hard on this cold case with Lauren. I'm thinking that any day now they're going to have answers that have been eluding the police for a long time."

It occurred to Ronny that Rich was good at making himself look like a hick or country bumpkin. Ronny would bet anything that the man was well educated, and that he had a head for things that others only dreamed about. It was a front, he thought, so that people would think they could take advantage of him, and that would be a mistake. Yes, he was a slick one, Rich McCullough was. Ronny would have to watch out for him. Smiling, he thought he was going to have fun being a part of the McCullough family.

Dinner was called an hour later. Ronny had to be brought his meals, as he was still laid up enough that he couldn't walk around on his own. And a wheelchair was fine for a little while, but it would hurt his back and he'd have to lie down after only a few minutes of being in one. He was trying to sit up in the chair when Jon was suddenly there to help him.

"I think it's about time, don't you?" He asked him what he meant. "To heal you so that you can be getting around. I think today would be a great day, don't you?"

"Yes, as a matter of fact, I do. I've been laid up here for long enough. And perhaps if I'm healed up a little more, my daughter won't treat me like I need a babysitter. She seems to think that I should wait until after the trial starts. I'm not one to sit idle when I can be moving around. So if you can fix me up, I'd like that." Jon asked him if he thought that was going to be true, that Reilly wouldn't worry about him so much. "No. I think I scared her a little. Scared me too, if you want to know the truth of it. I would appreciate any and all help you can give me, son. I surely would."

It only took him a moment to get himself sitting up to take the younger man's blood. And as soon as the elixir hit his system, Ronny felt like he'd put his wet finger in a live socket. He looked up at Jon and felt his world tilt a little, and found himself not just sitting up better on the couch, but he could actually sit up without any pain.

"You'll have to take it easy for a little while. At least a couple of hours." Ronny nodded, feeling like he had when he was younger and tried his hand at a little pot. "I'll help you to the dining room now. I think you'll enjoy sitting at the table for a change."

Ronny thought for sure that he could enjoy a great many things right now that he hadn't even before the accident. Looking at Jon, he felt a connection and smiled at him. This, he thought, was going to be the beginning of his new life. For some reason, Ronny wanted to change things around and spice them up. It was time that he started making himself as happy as his little girl was now.

Thanking Jon again, he wanted to skip to the table, he felt so good. But Ronny took his time, and was happy to know that he'd be able to stand up with Reilly tomorrow when she and Boyd became man and wife.

Chapter 13

Hawk kept himself close to the wall as he made his way to the elevator that would take him to the room that he'd rented for the day. He thought of Reilly as he tried his best not to freak out with all the other people around him. She'd done this—found the missing kid after only three days of doing a search. Well, they were all hoping it was him. Hawk was on the elevator when he heard from Reilly.

Okay, I'm not sure what this shit is that I have now, but can you tell me what the people look like that are standing around you? He described the six people in the elevator with him. He didn't even bother asking her what was going on. Hawk had enough shit going on now that nothing much surprised him anymore. *There should be a woman with a dog. I have no fucking clue why it's there, but do you see it?*

A dog? I would think that it would be having a meltdown about now with me in the elevator with it. She told him it wasn't really a dog. *Okay. I don't understand, but let me have a better look.*

The woman in front to his left had a dog in her arms. He wasn't sure that it was right. Hawk tried to get a closer look at the mutt, but she turned a little and he could see it laying across her arm. He told Reilly what he could see.

Okay, that's what I can see too. I've hacked into the cameras where you are, and I can see you all. Christ, what are they doing shoving you up against the wall there? Never mind. I'm going to stop the elevator. Bear with me, please. The elevator came to a sudden stop and he held tightly onto the railing surrounding them all. *Hawk, the police are on their way up to the floor that you're on. The dog is a child that just came up missing at the hospital.*

You're sure? Okay, don't answer that, you are. What do you want me to do now? She told him to just make sure that the woman didn't hurt the little girl. *I can do that. What does this have to do with the missing boy, if it's related at all?*

It is. She took young Emma there when she was six hours old. She's done the same thing before this, and I'm working on trying to find those children as we speak. Her bank accounts have been sealed up, thanks to Lauren. And she's going to back trace, if Lauren can do that, to see if she can find where the money came from. And I don't know why I even think that she can't.

She's selling them. It wasn't a question, but Reilly answered him as if it was. *What is it I can do right now? I don't want this child hurt any more than you do.*

Nothing for now. I'm worried that when the police show up there, she's going to hurt the child to get away. This has happened before, I'm afraid. He didn't ask her what had happened, Hawk loved kids too—when they were someone else's. *When the elevator moves, I want you to do something that will distract her. I don't know. Kiss her or something.*

192

Hmm, no thanks. But I'll see what I can do. He loved the women in his family, but Reilly, she held his heart a little tighter. He had no idea why—he got along with all of them—but he and Reilly could sit for hours, not saying a word, and be comforted by it.

The elevator started to move with a lurch, then stopped again. When it started moving smoother now, he thought of what he had to do in such a small space. Making his move now seemed the best possible time.

Bumping into the man next to him hard enough to knock him into the woman knocked her purse and cane to the floor. As he bent to pick it up, talking to her all the while, he moved himself into a better position. As soon as the doors opened, he was in a situation that he could not just grab the baby if things went south, but he was standing in front of her now instead of behind.

People moved out. Hawk was still trying to keep the woman inside with him when he heard the cops telling the two of them to put their hands up. As soon as the cop said that, she tossed the child into the air and drew a gun.

Hawk was able to hold the child while the others did what they had to do. The crime scene was a mess, but the child was safe, and that was all that mattered to them at the moment. The doctor was on his way to examine the child, then take her back to the hospital for tests and such. He was reasonably sure that the child had been drugged, and that frightened him a little.

Hawk had been feeling like he'd been run over three times and left in the sun to rot. Not just in the last few months, but even before that, he thought. His job had been boring, the

193

same thing over and over. He'd be called in to kill someone, take them to the police, or just find them. Today he'd felt needed, useful even. And as he sat there, waiting on the doc to come and see the child, he realized that he was also feeling lonely.

Hawk had been a loner all his life. Even as a child he would participate in activities, sports and things at school and with his family. But he didn't engage with them. Once whatever was going on was over, he would curl into himself and walk away. He wondered why he'd been that way a lot over the last few years, and thought it was too late for him to change.

Now he found that he not only wanted to change, but he also wanted to hang out more with his brothers. His sisters too. Because to Hawk, none of them were in-laws, but his sisters.

When someone touched his arm, Hawk's first reaction was to kill. Looking up at the man standing in front of him, it took him several seconds to get rid of the urges that had been as much a part of him as breathing. The man seemed to understand as he sat down next to him.

"Battle fatigue. I can recognize it on a fellow sufferer." He asked for the child, and when Hawk just stared at him, the man smiled. "I'm Doctor Cameron Scott. I've been sent here by Lauren McCullough to look over the child and to admit her to the hospital for observation. You should contact her."

"I'm sorry." He nodded and took the baby from him. Hawk watched him as he listened to her heart and checked her over from head to toes. When he was finished, Hawk told him again how sorry he was and tried to explain. "I've been military longer than I've been a civilian. I have to keep myself in control. My brother—he's a doctor too—he told me to write it all down. It's helped a lot."

"Good for him. When I first came home, it was difficult for me as well. People aren't like us." Doc Scott handed him the child. "You hold onto her. She's going to be just fine, but I'm to understand that there is a young man too that I should see."

"He doesn't know that the woman he was with is dead. I don't know how he'll take that. I've been unable to see him, as they've got him pretty much tied up with questions that apparently he's not answering for them." Doc Scott stood and asked him if he'd come with him, and to bring Emma, the little girl. "You need someone to protect you?"

"No, I think perhaps you might be able to help Mike better than I can. I want you to talk to him." He asked him if he knew what was going on. "Yes. When the door was broken down to the room, he was tied to the bed with a chain. There was no food or water near enough to him to get it—just out of his reach, as a matter of fact. I'm sure that she did that on purpose."

I have some information for you. Hawk told Lauren what he was doing before she could give him what she had. *Good. His name was Mike Raver. Now he goes mostly by Shithead. I kid you not, Hawk, if she wasn't dead already, I'd go there and kill her myself. You'd not believe the shit that Reilly has found since we have a name.*

I believe it. He entered the room as she was giving him a rundown on the stuff that the boy had endured. *I'm with him now, Hutch. He's like a wounded bear. That's all I can think of. Poor kid.*

He's going to need a lot of help before he's going to be all right. His parents have not been informed yet that we might have found him. I want to get him someplace where he can be examined and have blood work done before we tell them that this kid might not be theirs after all. Hawk handed Mike the baby when he reached for her, knowing that the kid had been doing this sort of thing for a long while. *She's taken at least three more babies that we know of at different hospitals across the state. Same way. She goes in, pretending to be the nurse for the nursery. Cuts all the monitors on the kid, strips it down to its bare skin, then drugs and dresses it. I've got some people working on her bank accounts. What's going on now?*

He's caring for the infant. Checking her diaper. Holding her in his arms and rocking her back and forth. Let me see what he's saying. Hang on. Mike was telling the child that she had to be quiet, that she'd be hurt if she wasn't. And that when she got to her new home, she was to remember him so that someone would love him when he was gone. He told Lauren what he said to the baby over and over. *Lauren, I think he believes that he was going to be killed today. I don't know why I think that, but he's just too defeated not to think that.*

That's what we think too. Hawk, this bitch stole some pretty heavy-duty drugs about two hours ago. Just before she took Emma. Hawk told Lauren that the doc said she was all right. *Good. I should have warned you he was coming. But I have shit going on here too. The woman's name is Shelly Weeks. Well, I guess it was Shelly Weeks. She actually pulled a gun on you? What the fuck is this world coming to when a nice man like you, who hadn't pulled his weapon yet, is accosted like that?*

He'd not been able to let any of the cops have the child; she seemed to need him as much as he needed her. As he was asked, several times, if he was all right, Hawk told them he was fine. Lauren must have ripped them a new ass, was all he could think about.

When Weeks tossed the baby into the air, Hawks first thought was it was a grenade. Then as his mind snapped into the present, he felt the first of many bullets enter his body. He only just managed to grab the child before she hit the floor. He was sure that she wouldn't have survived that, not as little as she was.

Weeks was pulling out another weapon when he grabbed her by the throat. His hand was tight around her, but she didn't struggle. He knew that this wasn't going to end with this bitch in jail. She'd hurt others and gotten away with it.

Tightening his grip on Weeks, he'd morphed his hand into a long blade and removed her head. It was that or she was going to get by him when he fell to the floor holding onto the infant. And since she'd put about a magazine of bullets in his body, he was sure that it would be labeled as self-defense. Or he hoped so.

He might not die from the wounds, but it sure as fuck hurt like hell. Falling to his knees first, he told the cops who he was, who he worked for, as well as his serial number and rank. Not that these men would give two shits about any of that, but the cell phone ringing in his pocket told him that Lauren or Reilly would save his ass from going to the chair.

They had treated him differently when the phone was put away. Hawk had still been lying on the floor, his wounds all but sealed up. He wondered what they would have done had they seen that the bullets seemed to push their way out of him and roll down the inside of his shirt. He thought they just might shit themselves.

"She was going to kill me today." He looked at the boy, Mike, when he spoke in a whisper. "I don't know how you knew I was in here, but I sure do appreciate it."

"You're so very welcome." He looked at the doc, and when he asked to be introduced to Mike, Hawk nodded and lifted the boy's face up to see him. "I've been held captive before too. It ain't pretty, is it?"

"No, sir. Are you going to give me away too? I don't want to go to that home." He asked him what home that was and Mike told him. As he relayed the information to Lauren, he wanted to go there now and take care of the place. "Nobody comes out of there when they use them all up."

"No, there is no way in hell you're going anywhere but to the hospital. Mike — your name is Mike, did you know that?" He said that he did, and he knew that he'd been kidnapped. "How?"

"She kept this book. And she made me look at it every day, telling me how my parents never searched very hard for me. If I ever have me a baby, I'm sure never gonna stop looking if somebody takes it." Hawk asked him if he knew the place where the book had been and if there were any other names in it. "Yes, sir. There are newspaper clippings of all the babies. She would make us read them every night before we went to bed."

Mike was examined, and he and Emma were taken to the hospital. Hawk stuck around. He knew that when Lauren had information for him, he was going to kill every adult in the place. Stretching his neck, feeling the pop of muscles when they stretched out, he was standing outside the hotel when she got back to him. He was going to his car even as she told him, several times, to stand down.

~~~

Jamie was sick. Not ill, but sick all the same. When she'd first started working here, she had wondered how they could pay her as much as they were and not have any customers. But as the days went by, she began to see the place for what it really was. At least she had a pretty good idea that she did.

Sneaking around hadn't been her strong suit while she'd been looking for the babies. She was better at coming up with excuses as to why she was someplace that she wasn't supposed to be. But today she knew just where they were, and she was going to take them out, even if she had to carry them in her clothing as she went.

The upstairs bedroom was off limits to her. In fact, all the upstairs was a place she'd been told not to go. But she was polishing the staircase when Ben said he was going to the store, and nodding when the door closed behind him, she ran as fast as she could up the two flights of stairs to the bedroom.

Now that she was where the babies were, she had to think what the fuck she might have been thinking. She didn't have a gun, but she knew that Ben did. So did Shelly. They were armed all the time, she'd found out, and that was what had scared her the most. But not enough to stop trying to find the children.

Jamie wasn't a sleuth or whatever she might have been called. But one night, not long ago, she'd gotten up to see if she had indeed locked up the cabinet with the cleaning supplies in it when she saw Ben and Shelly Weeks standing in the kitchen with a young couple.

It never occurred to her that this wasn't normal. That the couple had left the child in their care and was coming back for it. The Weeks ran a daycare, or so she had been told. Now she knew not only what the place was, but also that the children of the place were being held as sex slaves. Jamie was going to take care of them too. Just as soon as the babies were safe.

Getting closer, just to see what the infant had looked like, loving children of all ages, she heard what was really going on and her belly lurched up. They were selling them the child. And for a great deal of money too.

The conversation was about how they couldn't tell anyone where the child had come from, who had sold it to them, or anything else. If they did, Ben told the couple, not only would they lose the child, but their lives as well. He had pulled out a handgun, she supposed to make his point.

That had been three weeks ago. Now she was as close to finding them as she'd been able to. Jamie could hear them then, the pitiful wails of a baby. Her heart broke for it, and she doubled her efforts to find them.

She found the secret door and opened it just as she felt something touch the back of her head. Jamie wasn't stupid, she knew that she'd been caught and that it was a gun, Ben's gun, that was currently making its way into her brain. She didn't turn when he told her not to move.

"You don't listen very well, do you? I thought we told you several times, not to go snooping around. And what do I find? Not only were you someplace that you shouldn't have been, but you've gone and found the one place that we were hiding from you." Jamie told him that she just wanted the babies. "Not going to happen, I'm afraid. You're going to die, right along with that brat that's been living with us."

She had no idea who that might have been. The children, not the babies, were nowhere she'd been able to find them. And now it looked as if she never would. Jamie wanted to cry. She'd been so close.

The noise behind her had her turning. It was a mistake — she knew that as soon as she was pulled up against the front of Ben and he held her there. The gun to her head and his hand over her mouth made it impossible to beg the monster of a man in front of her not to kill her.

The gun in the man's hand looked tiny compared to his size. She thought perhaps he was some kind of shifter, but she had no idea. They'd told her once, a friend of hers who had been a wolf, that they were bigger in their human form for the other part of themselves. Jamie thought this guy must have had a lot of others in him. He grinned at the two of them, and Jamie felt the hairs on her arms dance. She'd was more afraid of the stranger than she was Ben. And he had a gun to her head.

"Let her go." Ben laughed and said that he wasn't going to do that. "No sweat off my balls. You kill her and you're still going to be dead. Purgatory is just waiting for another sick fuck like you."

She screamed behind the hand that covered her mouth. He'd just told Ben to kill her. What a fucking bastard. But there wasn't any way that she was going to be able to make him eat those words. Jamie was reasonably sure that she was going to be dead in the next few minutes.

"Your wife, I killed her earlier." Ben said that he'd not. "Yep. Cut her fucking head off where she stood, and still managed to save both Mike and Emma. As Mike told me what you'd done to him, I came right over to end your fucking miserable excuse for a life. You're just lucky that I don't have time to play. I would make you suffer in ways that you live through so that I could start again."

"Me and Jamie, we're going to leave here, and you're not going to do a thing about it. You move your ass out of the way and I'll tell you where the others are." The man shook his head and said no dice. "Then you're going to be responsible for this woman's life, as well as the other children that I have stashed."

"Fourteen twenty-four Market Street. There are seven kids there, all of them of varying ages under ten. You, mother fucker, are going to wish you'd never have been born when I'm done with you. Let the broad go, and you and I will just shoot each other until you're dead."

Jamie was getting mighty tired of this guy treating her like she wasn't anything but someone in his way. When she stomped her foot down on the top of Ben's foot, she heard the gun go off and the sting of something cutting her across her cheek. When she turned back to Ben, to.... Well, she wasn't sure what she was going to say to him, but it didn't matter. He was lying on the floor with a hole in his forehead. The other man touched her arm.

Jamie wasn't the violent type. She'd had enough of that during her childhood to know that fists never solved anything. But before she could think about the man's size and that he still had a gun in his hand, she doubled up her fist and hit him

202

right in his face. As he went down, she had a moment of fear, then she was pissed again.

"Get up." He said he was fine where he was. "No you're not. I want you to get up off that floor so that I can hit you again. You mother fucker, you told him to kill me. Then you... you...called me a broad. Then you...then you—"

Her belly lurched up and she leaned over and threw up twice before she could think that she was safe, and that the man on the floor was still in the room with her. When he stood up, she did the only thing she could think of and hit him again. This time in the balls.

The police seemed to be everywhere then. Jamie didn't think the man had even hit the floor again when she was being shoved up against the wall and cuffs put on her. All this for hitting that man that said it was all right with him if she was dead?

Jamie was asked her name and she told them she was James Fitzpatrick. When asked if she knew that was a man's name, she looked at the officer and asked him if he'd like his balls around his throat too. He stepped back from her when she struggled to do just that. She'd had enough of men for one day.

"Yes, I'm well aware that it's a man's name. It's been with me my whole life, you moron." The woman's laughter had her looking at the doorway. "Oh look, another broad that can be killed because that piece of shit has some sort of quota to fill."

"You're mouthy." He didn't look like he was pissed off any longer but told the cop to let her go. "If you don't, then I'm going to sic Lauren on you." The growl, loud and clear in the room, made her skin warm and her body respond. But not in a frightened way.

They didn't move. She was still sitting on the floor when the woman asked the man what was wrong with him. They both looked at her after they spoke quietly for a minute. Before she could ask what the hell they were talking about, the first baby was brought out of the passage way. Jamie went to mush, just like that.

"I said to let her go. I'm not going to tell you again."

Jamie looked at the big man, and she could swear that he'd gotten bigger. When no one moved still, she watched in horrific fascination as he shifted into the most beautiful creature she'd ever seen. Then his intent seemed to come to her. He was going to kill the cops.

Standing up while cuffed was harder than she'd thought it would be. Pushing her body between the dragon and the cops, she told him that she was going to murder him in his sleep if he harmed one more person today.

"Shift back to your other hulking self. You heard me. Right now." He didn't move, and she rammed her head into his belly before staggering back from it. "You're a bully and an asshole, and I said to shift back to the man. At least him I can talk to."

When the dragon licked his large fucking tongue over her cheek, she nearly came. It was the strangest feeling that she'd ever had. But he changed back to himself and stood there looking at her.

"You were going to kill those men." He said that he still might. "No you will not. If you can't behave yourself, then go into the hallway. I've had enough men bossing me around today. And you're still on my shit list."

The woman continued to laugh. Jamie didn't have any idea what the hell she found so funny, but she was distracted by the next two men that came into the room. They were related to the first man, and she'd just bet anything they were just as bossy. Suddenly she was free of the cuffs, and she looked at the three men.

They swallowed up the space in the room. And she'd bet any amount of money when people said for them to do something they did it. Jamie didn't have any delusions about the woman either. She just commanded authority.

The last few minutes caught up with her then. Sitting down on the floor she'd just gotten up from, Jamie saw the blood as it pooled under Ben's head. There was a lot, her scattered mind told her, and she looked at the man again. She couldn't seem to focus. And when someone asked her if she was all right, Jamie fell back and let darkness take her. Her last thought before she lost her grip was that she hoped to never see the man again.

Share your voice and help guide other readers to these wonderful books. Even if it's only a line or two your reviews help readers discover the author's books so they can continue creating stories that you'll love. Login to your favorite retailer and leave a review. Thank you.

AWARD WINNING, BESTSELLING AUTHOR

Kathi Barton, winner of the Pinnacle Book Achievement award as well as a best-selling author on Amazon and All Romance books, lives in Nashport, Ohio with her husband Paul. When not creating new worlds and romance, Kathi and her husband enjoy camping and going to auctions. She can also be seen at county fairs with her husband who is an artist and potter.

Her muse, a cross between Jimmy Stewart and Hugh Jackman, brings her stories to life for her readers in a way that has them coming back time and again for more. Her favorite genre is paranormal romance with a great deal of spice. You can visit Kathi online and drop her an email if you'd like. She loves hearing from her fans. aaronskiss@gmail.com.

Follow Kathi on her blog: http://kathisbartonauthor.blogspot.com/